"An Office Is An Awkward Place To Make Love— Too Many Interruptions,"

Matt murmured huskily.

He watched with interest when Kim's eyes narrowed, and continued, "And the timing was definitely wrong. We were there on business, and if things were going to work out, we had to wait."

"Wait?" she echoed breathlessly.

He nodded, moving closer. "Until our business was over."

"Matt, I hate to be the one to tell you this, but we've got the same reasons against doing this now that we had a week ago." She slid her hands to his chest and pushed. He was just like the table—he didn't budge.

"That's not the way I see it. Last week a business stood between us. Now it doesn't."

Kim wasn't afraid of Matt. She knew that if she told him flat out to let her go, he would. The major problem with that was that he felt good. Too good. And she couldn't quite get the words out. Three short syllables—let me go—and she just couldn't say them....

Dear Reader:

Welcome to Silhouette Desire! If you're a regular reader, you already know you're in for a treat. If this is your first Silhouette Desire, I predict you'll be hooked on romance, because these are sensuous, emotional love stories written by and for today's women—women just like *you!*

A Silhouette Desire can have many different moods and tones: some are humorous, others dramatic. But they *all* have a heroine you can identify with. She's busy, smart, and occasionally downright frazzled! She's always got something keeping her on the go: family, sometimes kids, maybe a job and there's that darned car that keeps breaking down! And of course, she's got that extra complication—the sexy, interesting man she's just met....

Speaking of sexy men, don't miss May's *Man of the Month* title, *Sweet on Jessie,* by Jackie Merritt. This man is just wonderful. Also, look for *Just Say Yes,* another terrific romance from the pen of Dixie Browning. Rounding out May are books by Lass Small, Rita Rainville, Cait London and Christine Rimmer. It's a great lineup, and naturally I hope you read them all.

So, until next month, happy reading!

Lucia Macro
Senior Editor

RITA RAINVILLE
PAID IN FULL

SILHOUETTE *Desire*®

Published by Silhouette Books New York

America's Publisher of Contemporary Romance

SILHOUETTE BOOKS
300 East 42nd St., New York, N.Y. 10017

PAID IN FULL

ISBN: 0-373-05639-7

First Silhouette Books printing May 1991

Printed in the U.S.A.

RITA RAINVILLE

has been a favorite with romance readers since the publication of her first book, *Challenge the Devil,* in 1984. More recently, she won the Romance Writers of America Golden Medallion Award for *It Takes a Thief*. She was also a part of the Silhouette Romance Homecoming Celebration as one of the authors featured in the "Month of Continuing Stars," and the Silhouette Romance Diamond Jubilee.

Rita has always been in love with books, especially romances. In fact, because reading has always been such an important part of her life, she has become a literacy volunteer and now teaches reading to those who have yet to discover the pleasure of a good book.

Southern California is home to this prolific and happily married author, who plans to continue writing romances for a long time to come.

To Lou, Marge and Barbara—
friends through thick and thin

One

Look before you leap.

How many times in her twenty-seven years had she been on the receiving end of that advice? Kim Cassidy wondered as she stared thoughtfully at the rough-hewn face of the man behind the large oak desk.

And how many times had she ignored it?

The score, she decided with a philosophical shrug, was about even. However, it was a bit late for regrets. If she hadn't learned the lesson by now, there wasn't much hope that she would. A pity, that. Because if ever a situation seemed to call for a bit of caution, this was it; if ever a man looked like the type to appreciate a more deliberate approach, it was Matthew Kingsley.

Matthew Kingsley.

He wasn't at all what she had expected the absentee owner to look like. Not that she had given the matter a great deal of thought, but if she had, she would have supposed that a man who owned a couple of hotels would be...well, older. Her gaze rested on the expensive, conservative cut of his dark brown hair as he stood up. He was probably about thirty-five.

And he was big.

Of course, looking at the world from the vantage point of five foot six made a lot of men look big. But he was. Undeniably. Big. Not that he was massive; he had the lean, muscular frame of a runner rather than the bulk of a linebacker. She estimated the top of her head wouldn't reach his chin, much less the steady gray eyes that had assessed her in the few seconds it had taken to walk from the door to his desk.

She took another quick glance at his squared-off chin and sighed. Yes, there was no doubt about it. Her aunts had pointed out the phenomenon years ago, and she had seen the truth of it proved again and again. That kind of chin generally belonged to a contrary, pigheaded man. A man who was usually hell on wheels.

Nor was there anything soft about the rest of his face. Heavy, dark brows matched the strength of his well-shaped mouth, and although the lean cheeks were smooth now, they would undoubtedly need a second shave before evening. Ah well, so much for her latest fantasy. She was definitely not dealing with an indulgent grandfatherly type here.

"Ms. Cassidy?"

She hadn't expected his voice to be so deep, either, but the intimidation factor matched everything else about him, she decided. Including his staff. His secretary was obviously cut from the same bolt of cloth. She had smiled pleasantly but said in a no-nonsense voice that Kim had exactly fifteen minutes.

Realizing that she had already wasted about forty-five seconds, Kim gave him a polite nod. "Thank you for seeing me on such short notice, Mr. Kingsley. I'll try not to keep you too long."

Settling into a high-backed chair across from his, she took in the dark blue suit that eased over his broad shoulders and flowed down to his long legs in knifelike creases. It was a work of art. She blinked at the perfection of his pale blue shirt and burgundy tie and decided that *he* was a work of art.

She waited patiently while his gray eyes did another quick survey, wondering idly if all high-powered executives were born knowing how to wield a business suit as a weapon. Or perhaps they took power dressing classes along the way. More than likely, she decided, they simply left everything to a high-priced tailor once they climbed that far up the corporate ladder.

Apparently satisfied, he leaned back and got right to the point. "What can I do for you, Ms. Cassidy?"

Kim grinned. She couldn't help it. She loved dealing with the bottom-line types. There was no shilly-shallying, no seesawing—just have at it. Forgetting all about caution and deliberation, she said cheerfully, "It's the other way around. I'm here to tell you that I'm the solution to your problem."

He took his time reading her expression. "I have a problem?" he asked finally.

"A whopper. If you have to ask, you're in more trouble than I thought." Kim leaned back and looked around the plush office. What she saw wasn't encouraging.

An oak file cabinet standing unobtrusively in a corner, and a sleek computer on his desk, were the only concessions to business that she could detect. The area, with its ivory walls and carpet and its slate blue chairs, was more reception room than office, but the imposing desk in the center indicated exactly who was in control. It didn't look like the office of a man who could be fast-talked or charmed into a business deal, Kim reflected wryly. That was a pity, because words and charm—and a great deal of talent—were all she had at her disposal.

Idly wondering where he kept the reams of paperwork that all businesses require, she studied a dark-framed landscape behind him. It was glorious, a series of soft, tree-studded rolling hills that reminded her of home.

The deep voice nudged her. "Maybe I should ask *which* problem?"

She turned back to him, meeting his steady gaze head-on. "Fair enough. It's not the missing sheets from house-keeping or the high-class call girl who's making a monkey out of security. I'm talking about the little jewel you're building on the top floor." She pointed a finger toward the ceiling. "The French country restaurant? The one where Henri is going to strut his stuff?" Had been going to strut his stuff, she amended silently. Yesterday the tempestuous chef had run off with Gerda, the stolid Swedish massage therapist. Today there was no Henri, and tomorrow there would be no country restaurant. Unless...

"Oh. That problem."

Kim nodded briskly. "But you're in luck," she assured him. "Yesterday when I heard about Henri, I started thinking. I—"

"*Where* did you hear about it?"

"In the kitchen. Anyway, when I heard—"

"What were you doing in the kitchen?"

Frowning impatiently, Kim said, "I work there. Anyway, with Henri gone I knew you'd—"

"Ms. Cassidy," he said evenly, "exactly who the devil are you?"

Kim stopped. A quick look assured her that he was serious. "I work for you," she said, astonished. "Sorry, I thought you knew. Back home we're on a first name basis with everyone for miles around, and I keep forgetting how different things are in the city. I'm one of your chefs, and I've been here almost four months now."

She paused, expecting him to comment. When he didn't she went on. "One of my specialties is the herbed omelets featured in the brunches. I'm very good." When his dark brows rose, she waited again politely, finally adding with a satisfied smile, "Whether you know it or not, you like my work. You just gave me a raise."

He seemed to sigh.

"Anyway, I had this idea. Now that Henri has jumped ship and you're just a couple of months away from the opening, you stand to lose a bundle of money if you don't think of something quick."

"I could always get another French chef," he murmured.

"Nope." She shook her head emphatically. "Not the caliber of Henri. He may be a bit impulsive—"

"Unreliable." His voice was hard.

"—but he's good," she finished breathlessly. "None of the other great ones are available right now. No, you have to take advantage of the talent you have on hand." She took a deep breath. "Fortunately for you, I'm on hand."

His sigh held a touch of impatience. "You're a French chef?"

"No." Kim shook her head again, brushing back strands of her long auburn hair and tucking them behind her ears. "But fortunately your decorator hasn't started on the restaurant yet. With hardly any changes at all, you can turn it into an *American* country restaurant, and I can show San Francisco just how good down-home cooking is."

"Wait a minute." He looked astounded. "You want me to turn it over to *you?*"

Kim shrugged, ignoring his incredulous tone. "Well, you don't seem to have a lot of options, and I am—"

"Don't tell me." He sounded resigned. "On hand."

Energy, Matt thought. That's what she was. Sheer, vibrant, sexy energy. He had felt it the second she stepped through the door in the dark green suit that somehow utterly refused to look businesslike. Even when she sat quietly, as she was doing now, zest radiated from her, ricocheted against the walls and zinged around the room.

When he saw her expectant expression he realized she was serious. For a split second he wondered how his ancestors—sober, stable and industrious businessmen to the core—would have reacted to her. Probably the way he was, with a blend of fascination and lust. And astonishment. Because if she believed that he would actually hand his new restaurant over to someone he had just met, she was as deluded as she was optimistic.

She had called it a jewel and she wasn't far off the mark. It was another glittering stone in the crown of Kingsley Towers, looking down on a city that was bustling and brash by day and shimmering like strands of brilliant gems at night. No, this wasn't a coffee shop they were discussing or some fast-food place that could change hands without a ripple. This was an intimate restaurant designed with a certain clientele in mind—people with money.

"Well, what do you think?"

Matt stared at her expressionlessly. She wasn't going to give up. He took his time about answering, eyeing the dark fire of her hair. It was cut in a wispy fringe straight across her forehead, emphasizing large green eyes that tilted upward slightly at the corners, then flowed straight down past her shoulders almost to her breasts. It was a style that would look angelic on a child—on her it was sexy.

It had been a long time since his body had gone on red alert at the sight of a woman, he reflected, but Ms. Kim Cassidy had gotten to him the instant she'd walked through the door. The slim skirt she wore had recorded the sleek length of her legs with every step she'd taken toward him. It had also clung to slim hips and what he assumed was a neat little bottom. Neither the fitted suit jacket nor the soft blouse underneath hid the high, small breasts. Matt's gaze touched the tempting mouth that was soft with humor, then lifted fractionally to take in eyes gleaming with intelligence. Kim shimmered with enthusiasm and a barely leashed desire to skip the basics and get on with the main event.

He suddenly wondered if she made love with the same reckless abandon. Speculation narrowed his eyes. Another look at the eagerness beneath her self-imposed calm convinced him. Yes, she probably did. If a man didn't take control right from the start, she'd probably—

Kim cleared her throat, bringing his attention back to the business at hand. Business, he reminded himself, meeting her curious gaze.

"Do you always take this long to answer a question?" she asked.

"Are you always this impulsive?" He fought a smile as a rueful expression crossed her face.

Sighing, Kim considered the question. It was inevitable. But it had to be answered. After all, she thought with a surge of enthusiasm, if they were going to work together it wouldn't remain a secret for long. "Well, yes, as a matter of fact I am."

With a look of genuine curiosity Matt asked, "Have you ever thought of trying a different approach—like gradually leading up to a subject? Tiptoeing over heavy ground?''

"You mean practicing the gentle art of negotiation? Of course, I have." She considered the matter for all of ten seconds then shook her head. "But as far as I'm concerned, it's just a waste of time."

Matt wondered why he wasn't surprised.

"Look at it this way," she instructed, leaning forward and tapping a slim finger on the rounded edge of his desk. "If I came in here and talked about everything except the one thing that interests us both, you'd end up wondering what on earth I was doing here, and we would have wasted a perfectly good meeting. On top of that, I would probably never have gotten another appointment with you."

"No," he said clearly. "You're wrong there. You would definitely have been invited back."

Kim tilted her head, her eyes narrowing. Rash she might be, but she wasn't stupid. Although he hadn't uttered a chauvinistic word, if the sudden gleam in his smoky eyes was any indication, he definitely wasn't thinking about wheeling and dealing. At least not with restaurants. Without giving the matter another thought she tumbled into speech.

"Oh, no, *please*. Give me a break, okay? Let's not play that game." She didn't even try to hide her exasperation. Few things annoyed her as much as being on the receiving end of a loaded glance like that while she was working. Masculine appreciation was all well and good, but there was a time and place for everything—and here and now wasn't it.

Stopping long enough to grab a breath, she rolled on. "It's beyond me why a man and woman can't have a business discussion without it sliding into...something like this." She eyed him severely and waved an impatient hand that seemed to encompass "this." "Let's understand each other, Mr. Kingsley. I'm a cook. A darned good one. I came in here to discuss the restaurant. What we have going on here is a business meeting. Our personal lives are entirely separate. I never try seduction to get what I want, nor do I allow myself to be seduced to settle for what I *don't* want."

Skidding to a halt, Kim took a deep breath and eyed his impassive face uncertainly. This might just make the famed Guinness book for the fastest business meeting on record, she reflected, wondering how long it would take him to lose his temper. He looked like a man who had a nasty one, and God only knew she had just given him enough provocation. Wondering how many bridges she had just burned, Kim thought again about looking and leaping. Yes, she definitely had to work on it.

She cleared her throat and stared at him, refusing to be the first one to look away. But it would be nice if he said something to break the loaded silence, she thought wistfully. Anything.

"Got that out of your system?" he finally asked.

She nodded.

"Good." He gave her a level look that cooled her down as quickly as she had flared up. "I don't usually mix my business and personal life, either, Ms. Cassidy. When we're through, my decision will be based on whether or not I think you can run a restaurant. Understood?"

Kim nodded again, relieved by both his level tone and his statement. The feeling was short lived. At the sudden speculation in his eyes she stiffened, waiting for the other shoe to fall.

"And as you said," he murmured blandly, "anything else that happens between us will be entirely separate from business."

Kim stared at him, her mouth half-open in protest. That wasn't what she had said at all. At least she didn't think it was.

"Now," he said briskly, "tell me about yourself and why you think you can run a restaurant."

Still mulling over his last disturbing comment, she rattled off her educational background, her three-year apprentice program with a prestigious hotel in Los Angeles and the various awards she had won. "That brings me to this year," she concluded. "Just before I came here, I spent a few months at my family's herb farm working on new recipes."

"Herb farm?"

She gestured vaguely. "North of here. Inland a little. It was wonderful—all the herbs I needed were at my disposal." She grinned. "Free."

Matt frowned, thinking about what she had said earlier. She was right. He *should* have known her. It was just another indication that the operation was getting too big. He had once known every employee in the hotel on a first name basis; now he was barely able to keep up with the managers.

"I wasn't taking advantage of them," she pointed out, blinking at his dark frown. "I did my share of the work, and they got to eat the food. My aunts don't like to cook, and Uncle Theo likes nothing better than having a woman put a plate of food in front of him. Believe me, everybody was satisfied with the arrangement."

Matt nodded absently, not sure what her relatives had to do with the discussion. "The fact that you work here tells me that you can cook," he said abruptly. "How good are you?"

Kim didn't hesitate. "Superb," she said coolly. "You're lucky to have me."

His eyes narrowed. "And you think you can handle the business end?"

She gave him a level look. "I know I can. Otherwise I wouldn't be here."

Now it was Matt's turn to stare. The delectable Ms. Cassidy was as intrepid as she was rash. That she didn't back down intrigued him. She just waited, eyeing him with anticipation while he thought it over. "Prove it," he challenged softly.

Kim blinked, surprised but undaunted. "How?"

"Cook dinner for me."

"If you want to sample my cooking, all you have to do is ride down to the main floor and walk into the Pyramid Room," she pointed out in a reasonable tone. "I work there five days a week."

"I don't mean here, where everything's at your disposal and four other chefs are hovering around."

Eyeing him with dawning appreciation, she asked, "Exactly where *do* you mean? Somewhere like my house?" Her hair brushed her shoulders like a silken scarf when she tilted her head.

Matt sighed sharply, pushed back his chair and got to his feet. Walking over to the large window, he glared down at the traffic. What the hell was he doing? She wasn't the manager he was looking for. He had known that the second she'd opened her mouth. Even if she lived up to the intelligence gleaming in those bewitching eyes, she was far too open. She looked too gullible. The staff and the vendors would eat her for breakfast the first day. Henri had a tongue as sharp as his favorite carving knife, and that's exactly what he wanted, not someone he'd have to baby-sit.

"Forget it," he told her briskly, lifting his gaze beyond the buildings to the sparkling Pacific Ocean. "I was out of

line. In fact, Ms. Cassidy, I think we'd be better off if we
forgot the whole thing.''

"Wait a minute!" Kim jumped to her feet and joined
him at the window. She looked up at him, her face alight
with enthusiasm. "I think it's a brilliant idea. In fact I was
going to suggest it. You're right, you know. It wouldn't be
fair to do it here at the hotel with the other cooks around.''
She took another quick breath. "You name the night.''

"Ms. Cassidy—"

"Kim." She waved an impatient hand. "You aren't
going to keep calling me Ms. Cassidy when I'm managing
the restaurant, are you?''

She was serious. Not knowing whether to laugh or
swear, he settled for shoving his hands in his pockets and
asking, "Do you ever slow down?''

"Besides," she rushed on, "you don't call Henri Mr. La
Porte, do you?" She ignored his frown and assured him,
"Of course you don't. No one does. Henri is Henri. And
I'm Kim." Her smile was brilliant. "Now, what night?
Your calendar is probably fuller than mine so it's up to
you. I'm free every evening this week except tonight.''

Matt could no more resist the pull of her excitement than
he could have fought his way out of a tidal wave. It had
been too long, he realized. Too long since he had been with
a woman so filled with energy and determination. Too long
since one had swept him away with her enthusiasm and
sheer joy. Too long since desire had tied him up in knots
when a woman walked into the room. Spending an evening with her was a temptation he couldn't resist.

Well, hell, he thought ruefully, so much for good intentions. Wondering why she wasn't free that evening, he
made up his mind.

"Tomorrow night." He didn't bother looking at his
calendar; whatever he had on tap he'd cancel.

"Seven?"

"Seven."

"Chicken or fish?"

"Fish." He eyed her thoughtfully. "What if I said beef?"

"You wouldn't get it. I don't think red meat is healthy. I don't fix it for anyone." She rummaged through her black shoulder bag and triumphantly pulled out a small card. "Here's my address." Holding it out to him, she smiled and said, "Tomorrow."

"Seven," he agreed, holding the card and watching her walk to the door. Her fiery hair, sleek and straight as a waterfall, touched the middle of her back. His gaze dropped to the slim skirt. Yes, a very neat bottom. A very sexy neat bottom.

When the door closed, Matt absently loosened his tie, unbuttoned the top button of his shirt and looked at the card. Crisp and businesslike, it simply noted her name, address and telephone number. It told him none of the things he had learned in the past fifteen minutes. A grin tugged at his mouth. It could easily have said: Kim Cassidy; Chef, Unmitigated Optimist, Fastest Tongue in the West, Sexy Lady. And beneath that chatty facade, he'd lay odds she was also one sharp, savvy lady.

She came from a place where people knew everyone for miles around, called them neighbor.

Did she know how lucky she was?

Obviously not. If she did, she wouldn't be living and working in the heart of San Francisco.

His gaze shifted to the wall, to the landscape she had examined so thoroughly with what seemed to be a vague sense of recognition. It was hung there behind his desk for a very good reason: serene as it was, he found it too distracting to look at every time he glanced up. It was an idyllic scene, perfect. Too perfect. He doubted if it actually existed, but it had come to be a symbol of...of what? Escape? Refuge? He shrugged impatiently. Whatever, it was a place where he could mentally retreat when the city became too noisy, too suffocating.

He had no idea who the artist was; he'd bought it on a whim. Then he'd hung it in his office for the same reason. Walking over to it, he smoothed the polished wood frame with his fingertips, frowning absently. Lately he'd spent too much time staring at the rolling hills, wondering if such a place did exist, if he could find it. Well, if he ever did, if he ever actually went there, he wouldn't arrive empty-handed. He had a drawer full of plans—and dreams—to take along with him.

He stroked his thumb along the frame one last time and went back to his desk. Pressing a button on the intercom, he said, "Mary, would you call personnel and ask them to send up everything they have on Kim Cassidy?"

"Sure thing, Matt."

"Thanks. Oh, and cancel whatever I've got scheduled for after six tomorrow night." He swung his chair back to face the picture, staring at it thoughtfully. Mary was not only cheerful, she was competent. He knew he would have the material within the hour. While he waited he mulled over one of the many puzzles of Kim Cassidy.

A chef who wouldn't prepare beef?

"Hi, Jock." Kim smiled at the thin, middle-aged man balanced comfortably on the ladder. His jeans, shirt and shoes were speckled with a rainbow of colors. A billed hat protected his wiry gray hair from the same polka-dot effect. Her landlord was retired and spent most of his time adding sparkling coats of paint to his pride and joy, one of the city's "painted ladies."

The beautifully restored Victorian homes added their own dash and color to a multiethnic, multicultural city, and Kim knew that for several reasons she was fortunate beyond belief. First, she had actually found a rental in a nice area. An affordable one. Second, the house was large and rambling, there was a carport for her small car, and her half of the second floor included the turret. Actually the turret was a bonus; she had chosen that apartment because it had boasted a small but efficient kitchen.

Jock Trent and his wife, Margo, suffering from the empty-nest syndrome when she'd answered their ad, had welcomed Kim as if she were the daughter who had just married and moved across the country. They were tactful and thoughtful landlords, and to show her appreciation Kim frequently fixed dinner for them, usually in their kitchen.

Now she shaded her eyes and watched as Jock carefully traced a wooden filigree. He lowered the brush so she could see it. "Like it?"

Kim moved closer. "Gorgeous color. It looks like the salmon I'm going to fix for dinner tomorrow."

He looked alarmed. "We're not going to be here tomorrow."

"I was counting on that," she said heartlessly. "My boss is coming over. It's for him."

He almost dropped the brush. "You did it?"

"Oh ye of little faith. Of course I did it." She grinned at his stunned expression. "I said I was going to invite him if things worked out, didn't I?"

"You say a lot of things." His voice was dry. "How'd you swing it?"

"He challenged me. After that, as my friend Henri would say, it was a *fait accompli*."

Jock looked at her thoughtfully. "So the little French guy really took off with the massage therapist?"

"Yep." She ducked a drop of paint. "Eloped. The grapevine has it that she was going on vacation, and he decided he couldn't live without her for a month." She shook her head. "I never thought he'd do it."

"Sex," he pronounced solemnly, squinting at his drying brush, "is a weird and wonderful instinct. It motivates people to amazing and quite unprofessional actions."

Kim grinned up at him. "Thank you, professor, I'll remember that. Especially when I'm around my boss." A sudden memory of his level gaze made her realize that she wasn't entirely joking. Hell on wheels, she reminded herself, clinging to the thought as if it were a mantra. And trouble. Lots of it.

Jock shot her a quick look. "I take it he's not the paunchy, gray-haired type you were expecting." Her rueful expression told him all he needed to know. Abruptly serious he asked, "Will you be okay with him tomorrow night? Alone?" While she blinked at the unexpectedly hard edge to his voice, he added, "We can stay home."

"Jock! Don't even think about it. I'm kidding. I'll be fine, just . . . fine," she ended lamely, getting another narrowed glance for her efforts.

He squinted down at her. "You're sure?"

Her pause was almost imperceptible. "Absolutely," she said in a precise tone. "It's simply a business meeting. I'm here to make a splash in the big city, remember? Small-town girl makes good and all that stuff? I want my picture in all the glossy food magazines. To be known. My motto is: San Francisco Today, Tomorrow, the World!"

"The Alexander the Great of chefs?"

"Exactly." She gave an emphatic nod.

"And you don't miss your family? The herb farm?"

"Of course I do," she said finally. "But I'm where I need to be...for now."

Jock got down from the ladder and neatly collected his paraphernalia. "Okay, so you don't need a baby-sitter tomorrow night. Want to use our kitchen?"

"I thought you'd never ask." She picked up a paint can and trailed along behind him to the utility shed. "Yes, definitely, I'll need to spread out a bit."

"You got it. I'll tell Margo."

A serene voice behind them asked, "You'll tell Margo what?"

Kim handed the paint can to Jock and turned to the plump, graying woman. "That my boss is coming to dinner and I need your kitchen."

With a shriek of excitement Margo threw her arms around Kim and gave her a swift hug. "You *did* it?"

Kim grinned. "I did it."

"Tell me all about it, every word. When's he coming?"

"Tomorrow night."

With a grunt, Jock sealed the lid on the can. "Ask her what he's like."

Years of reading between the lines had Margo demanding instantly, "What's he like?"

Kim lifted one shoulder in a negligent shrug, both amused and touched by their concern. "Younger and tougher than I expected." Sexier. And far more dangerous.

"Uh-oh." Margo checked silently with her husband, then gave Kim a long look that vibrated with maternal suspicions. "You want us to stick around when he comes?"

Smiling, Kim shook her head. "Absolutely not. I'm twenty-seven, remember? Besides, Jock already offered. Just your kitchen, please."

"You got it," Margo told her, slipping an arm around Kim's waist and turning toward the house. "Now, I want to hear all about the famous interview. Don't leave out a word. But first tell me about the big boss."

"Well, you're right on that point," she said lightly. "He *is* big. And he has incredibly sexy gray eyes."

"Anything else?" Margo's voice was dry.

"Um. Unfortunately. He looks like he should be out trapping wild animals instead of sitting behind a desk." She stopped, staring absently at a clump of white peonies. "No, actually, he looks like one of the wild animals."

Margo groaned. "I just married off my last daughter. I thought I didn't have to worry about predatory males any more." Touching Kim on the shoulder she said, "I hope you have your running shoes handy."

Two

He was early.

Matt checked the wide gold watch on his wrist again as he eased into one of the few remaining parking spots on the narrow street.

Too early.

If he had any sense he wouldn't even be here. Especially since he had already made up his mind that there was no way in hell he was going to put his restaurant in Kim Cassidy's soft little hands. He didn't care how talented she was or how hard she was willing to work, she just didn't have the experience or the discipline for the job. She also lacked prudence. And she wasn't tough enough. The list was endless.

He automatically turned the front wheels into the curb and switched off the ignition. He should have called and told her. Well, he had tried. Twice he had actually picked up the phone—and twice he had cradled it again. She would be disappointed, and he knew that her dismay would be reflected in her expressive eyes. And that was why he was here, he told himself. To deliver the bad news in person and help pick up the pieces afterward.

He grinned. Who was he kidding? The very traits she lacked for business were the ones that had brought him to her house tonight, as well as the dinner invitation and the business discussion, he reminded himself.

There was no shortage of seasoned female executives in his life. What was definitely in short supply was a woman who wore trust and enthusiasm like a banner, whose femininity and humor gleamed in the depths of her green eyes. A woman whose zest for life intrigued him as nothing else had in a long, long time.

He locked the car and looked around the well-kept neighborhood. She had chosen well, he decided. In this part of town, Kim would be as safe as any woman could be in a big city. As he started down the hill, his mind circled back to the thought that had nagged at him for the past twenty-four hours: what was missing in his life was a special woman. Before the night was over, he promised himself, he would know if he had found her, if Kim Cassidy was her name.

Matt checked the number on the gate and stopped, a smile tugging at the corners of his mouth. The pampered yellow house practically preened, its avocado trim exuberantly highlighting the peaked roof and showing off its turret with pride. It sat squarely on its foundation, undisturbed by the steep slant of the street. The yard, generous by San Francisco's standards, looked like an English country garden. Waves of pink, purple and blue flowers—none of them roses, he noted—were punctuated by alternate splashes of white and yellow.

It was the kind of house an incurable optimist would live in, he decided. Bright, cheerful, all banners flying. It didn't look any more susceptible to rejection or defeat than Kim had yesterday in his office. It had the same air of resilience that she did.

It wasn't going to be easy to tell her.

The sudden realization jolted him to a stop, his hand coming to rest on a pointed slat of the white picket fence.

Easy?

Hell, it was going to be all but impossible. She didn't react the way other people did. She didn't even listen the way other people did. His experience with her so far only proved one thing: there was nothing predictable about Kim Cassidy. He was staring at the house, wondering how he could have overlooked such a vital point, when Kim threw open the oak door and stepped out on the wide, wrap-around porch.

"Hi. You're early."

"You're right." He glanced automatically at his watch then loped up the stone stairs. "Ten minutes. If it's a problem, I can sit on the porch swing while you pretend that I'm not here." His level glance told her she'd be in trouble if she tried.

He wanted to be where he could watch her. Kim's understated pale pink dress, with its long sleeves and modest neckline, shouldn't have been provocative, and maybe it wasn't—on a coat hanger—but with the silky fabric drifting over her curves and brushing her slim legs each time she moved, it was tantalizing. But then, he reflected with grim acceptance, he seemed to find everything about Kim tantalizing.

She smiled and waggled an inviting hand. "Don't be silly. You're going to come in and be dazzled by my efficiency. Not only am I an exceptional cook," she informed him cheerfully, "I'm very well organized."

Matt tore his gaze from her teasing expression, reminding himself that as far as Kim was concerned, this was strictly a business meeting. The fact that he should regard it the same way was briefly considered. All right, he allowed. Business. As well as personal.

He surveyed the pale gold rooms as he followed her into the updated version of a formal parlor. Silly? he wondered. How many years had it been since someone had tossed that word in his direction? More than he could remember, he decided after a few seconds' thought.

He took another, slower look around. "Nice house."

"Nice?" Kim tested the word. "It's beautiful! Unfortunately I can't take any credit. Well, maybe a little for the yard, but otherwise the house is owned by a doting couple who spoil it rotten." A wave of her hand indicated the sun-filled room. "The inside is all like this. Light and airy with clean lines, and yet they've kept all the gorgeous old gingerbread stuff on the outside. The best of both worlds, as I see it." She dropped lightly into a dark green chair and waved him to its mate. "My apartment is upstairs."

"It looks like you have the run of the whole place," he commented, watching her fingertips absently trace a pattern over the carved chair arm.

"Yep, I do. Reciprocity is the name of the game," she said with a satisfied nod. "I occasionally cook for them, and they let me use their kitchen."

"They're getting the best of the deal."

"I never let them forget it," she assured him. "After all, not everyone is fortunate enough to have a Kingsley Tower chef on the premises. Or the manager of a cozy little country restaurant."

When his eyes narrowed she shook her head and uttered a small disgusted sound. "Sorry. I told myself I wasn't going to do that. It isn't fair—to you or to me."

"Kim—"

She shook her head. "No, it's totally unrealistic to expect you to say anything until after you've eaten. There'll be plenty of time to talk business then."

Matt's sigh was a sharp sound in the pleasant room. "Kim, I really need to—"

She held up her hand, palm facing him. "No. You don't. I understand." She nodded to a small bar in the corner, effectively changing the subject. "Would you like a drink?"

Matt shook his head. "Thanks, no." There were a lot of things he needed right now, but a drink wasn't one of them, not if he was going to stay one step ahead of her.

Ahead? he reflected ruefully. At the rate he was going, he'd be lucky to even keep up with her. Doing business with Kim was like dealing with a handful of pups all hellbent on going in different directions. The moment you had one under control, four others were frisking around getting into trouble.

Kim's problem, he decided moodily, was that she didn't take business seriously. She apparently hadn't learned that in the corporate world levity often came across as irresponsibility. If she wanted to run her life on impulsive and rash decisions, that was fine with him. She could do what she wanted *when* she wanted. Hell, he'd even help her—he could use a little spontaneity in his life—as long as his new restaurant wasn't involved.

Unfortunately, in this particular situation, Kim's problem was *his* problem because he was where the buck stopped. He handled the bad along with the good, and most of the time he handled it well. Tough decisions were just a part of the job. They had to be made every day. But most of them were impersonal, usually based on computerized data. This was different. This time when he said no he'd have to watch the light fade from a pair of hopeful green eyes.

"You're looking awfully grim," Kim observed, eyeing his frown with one of her own. "I didn't ask you over here to poison you, you know. This is supposed to be fun—even if it is business." When his expression didn't lighten she asked with sudden suspicion, "What time did you eat lunch?"

"Hmm?" Matt lifted abstracted eyes.

"Lunch," she prompted. "When?"

"I don't think I had any."

Kim stared at him then shifted her gaze upward. "I don't believe this," she told the ceiling in an exasperated tone. "My whole career is at stake, hanging by a thread. And it's hanging in front of a man who's probably hungry enough to chew the thread." Sighing dramatically she got up and crooked her index finger in a "follow me" gesture. "Come on, let's go to the kitchen before you start nibbling on the hand that's about to feed you."

She walked to the far door and stopped, looking over her shoulder to make sure he was still with her. Matt was dressed in another power suit, dark gray this time. She had taken in the lean, casual threat of him in one sweeping glance when she'd opened the door, and now she was suddenly aware of just how much elegantly covered hard muscle was right behind her, much closer than she had expected. The thought did nothing to settle her nerves.

All right, she admitted silently as she waved him to a chair at the oval table, she was not as calm as she'd like to be. Calm? Her hands stilled while she considered the statement. At least no one could accuse her of exaggerating, she decided. It wasn't cooking a meal for him that bothered her—that part was a piece of cake. She wasn't even particularly worried about the outcome of the evening. It was just that Matthew Kingsley made her... nervous.

Kim concluded she was entitled to a few qualms. After all, she hadn't been exposed to such a dose of blatant masculinity, however subtly it was covered, since high school when she'd suffered through a brief but tumultuous infatuation with a motorcycling rebel in black leather. Her uncle and two aunts hadn't been unduly concerned, she remembered. They had relied on her common sense to bring her through the experience unscathed, and that was exactly what had happened. Loaded glances and heavy breathing had eventually lost their appeal. That had been almost ten years ago. But apparently some things just didn't change with time, Kim mused, because she felt as woefully unprepared now as she had been then.

She dropped a large white apron over her head and tied it snugly at her waist before removing two marinated salmon steaks from the refrigerator. It wasn't as if she had been hibernating during these years. She had dated a number of pleasant men, had even been engaged to one of them for a brief time. But not once in all those years had she run into a prowling, hungry-eyed man like Matthew Kingsley. And now, even as inexperienced with the type as she was, it was obvious that whether they wore black leather or sleek, expensive suits, men like Matthew spelled one thing.

Trouble.

Kim brought her mind back to the present problem and reached up to pull a box from the oak cupboard. She handed Matt a few crackers. "Here, eat them slowly. That's all you're going to get." Sliding the salmon in the high tech broiler, she said chattily, "Both of the Trents like to cook, so this room has every gadget known to man and the gourmet shop in the mall. When they remodeled they had to cut corners in several places, but not, thank God, in here."

She turned back just as Matt downed the last cracker and began eyeing the box with predatory intent. Hastily stuffing it back in the cupboard, she said, "Sorry, I'm not going to let you spoil your appetite. Those were just to take off the edge. I want your full attention on this meal. After all, how am I going to make San Francisco sit up and take notice if I can't impress one man?"

Matt unbuttoned his jacket and leaned back in the chair. "Is that what you want, to be famous in San Francisco?"

The sound of his deep voice ruffled her nerve endings. Annoyed with her reaction, she reached for several rosy new potatoes and a sharp knife. The wicked blade flashed and the potatoes slid aside in uniform slices. Satisfied with the results, she looked up with a small smile. "It's a start."

"You're ambitious." His gray gaze followed her brisk movements.

"Don't make it sound like an indictment. I'm proud of it." Kim removed a stainless steel dish of torn greens from the refrigerator and set it on the center island. "That's why my address is San Francisco instead of Posy Creek." And if she had occasional moments of doubt about the move, it was none of his concern, she reminded herself.

"You're kidding." He looked intrigued. "Posy Creek? The place where everyone is on a first name basis for miles around?"

"All five hundred of them," she told him, her face softening.

He took in the warmth of her small smile. "You like the place."

Amazement deepening the green in her eyes, Kim said earnestly, "Of course, I do. There's nothing *not* to like about Posy Creek." Energetically whisking a creamy salad dressing, she said, "It's a bit like Camelot."

When his dark brows rose, she considered her words thoughtfully, then nodded, affirming them. "Really. It's true. The sun shines just the right amount and we get exactly enough rainfall, both for the crops and to keep the mountain air clean. There's not a trace of smog. In the morning, birds not traffic wake you up, and later, people stop whatever they're doing just to watch the sunsets.

"The town is small, and the people are happy and healthy," she ended simply, putting aside the whisk and turning her attention to a plate of fresh asparagus.

"How small?"

Her sudden grin charmed him. "One main street, two blocks of stores and no traffic lights. The heaviest traffic of the day is when the kids get out of school."

"Sounds nice."

Her eyes soft with memories, she nodded. "More than nice. Cassidys have lived in Posy Creek for four generations." She opened the broiler door and peeked at the salmon. "Someday, probably when I'm ready to retire, I'll go back. I have a house there, you know." He made an encouraging sound and she explained. "When my parents died, they—"

"How long ago was that?"

"About fifteen years ago. They left the house in trust for me. It's a half mile from the family herb farm." Kim touched a loaf of freshly baked bread with her finger, testing the temperature. "My aunts thought it was important for me to stay in my own home, so they moved out of the house they shared with Uncle Theo and in with me. That's how we lived until a few years ago, when I finished college and was accepted at the culinary academy. Then they went back to their own house and Uncle Theo. Now when I go back to visit, I stay in my place and just walk down the road to see them."

Keeping a watchful eye on the broiler, steamer and microwave, Kim tossed the salad. Even when the pace picked up, her words remained unruffled. Several minutes later she put the assorted dishes on the table, removed the apron and slid into the chair across from Matt. Laying her napkin in her lap, she commanded, "Eat."

"Only once in the past year have I eaten a meal that good." Matt touched the napkin to his mouth and watched Kim take a swallow of coffee. During the meal there hadn't been a trace of concern on her expressive face; the lady knew she was good.

"Thank you." A small frown knit her russet brows. "Who cooked the other one?"

His smile warmed her. "Another genius."

"Ah." It was almost a purr of satisfaction. "Nicely put, Mr. Kingsley."

"Matt."

"Matt?" She said the word slowly, thoughtfully. "All right," she said finally, making her resistance clear. "For right now. Tonight. But not at the hotel."

"Why not?"

"Because everyone in the kitchen calls you Mr. Kingsley, that's why."

"Not Henri."

"Maybe you haven't noticed, but I'm not Henri."

Matt scowled. "I've noticed." He didn't give a tinker's damn what everyone else called him. He wanted her soft lips curving and closing around his name.

She had been right yesterday, Kim decided, taking another quick look at his face. The determined look in his eyes perfectly matched the set of his square chin. Stubborn. Yes indeedy. And this time it was just over a name. He looked ready to dig in his heels and argue the point. Well he could argue all he wanted to. She was right and she knew it. Whether or not he wanted to acknowledge it, there was a certain protocol to be observed. While she was still mulling that over, he surprised her again.

"What did you marinate the salmon in?" he asked abruptly.

Kim blinked. Amusement replaced the stubborn resistance behind the curtain of her dark lashes. "Hasn't anyone ever told you that a chef's recipes are guarded like the family jewels?"

A grin tugged at his lips. "Yeah, I've heard that. Was fennel in it?"

"Nope." She shook her head, relaxing enough to return his smile.

Matt's gaze followed the lazy slide of her hair over her shoulders, and he fought a sudden compulsion to catch it in his hand, to tangle his fingers in the fiery, fragrant mass. Instead he responded to her amused glance with another question. "Coriander?"

"Nope." She relented a bit. "I used orange juice as a base, but that's all you're going to get."

That's what you think, lady, he thought. And swift as lightning in a summer storm, his body tightened until he could hardly breathe. She was wrong. Dead wrong. He was going to get it all. He was going to get her.

Kim stood and deftly stacked the plates. "Don't get up," she said quickly. "I'm just going to put this stuff in the sink. I'll clean up later." There was no need to tell him that what she really needed was space—a lot more than what the small table offered.

When he followed with the remaining dishes Kim caught her breath. The closer he came, the more the large kitchen seemed to shrink, and although he wasn't touching her, he was too close, too big. And he was crowding her.

He wasn't doing it deliberately, she assured herself after a quick glance at his bland face. She just wasn't accustomed to working in such close quarters with a man like Matt. Working with men, yes; she had done that for years. But they were simply other cooks, people who shared her talent. Unfortunately for her shredded nerves, Matt didn't fall into that neutral, comforting category.

"You wash and I'll dry," he told her, shrugging out of his jacket and rolling his sleeves to his forearms. When he snagged a folded towel and leaned against the counter, she gave a small shrug and decided to save her strength for the discussion that was still ahead of them.

Handing him a plate, she asked curiously, "Have you always lived in San Francisco?"

"Matt," he prompted.

Kim sighed. Stubborn. No doubt about it. "Matt," she agreed reluctantly.

He nodded, not a trace of his satisfaction creeping into his voice. "Yeah. Except for a few years in the service. My family is as rooted in the city as yours is in Posy Creek. Three generations of us."

Eyeing his face suspiciously, Kim decided that Matt was a better winner than she was a loser. He didn't look like a man who had just aced a major point. He also had a dish-drying technique that raised the mundane task to an art. He handled the plate as if it were the Holy Grail. She turned to get a better view, watching in utter fascination as he dried every inch of it several times then held it up to the light to make sure there were no streaks.

Did he handle a woman with that same rapt, narrow-eyed concentration?

Kim blinked at the unexpected thought as she watched his large, well-shaped hand slide the towel over the plate. With his prominent brows and high cheekbones he definitely wasn't the soft, pretty type, she reflected, sliding an oblique glance in his direction. As far as that went, most women probably wouldn't even consider him handsome. He was a lot more basic—and dangerous—than that. Matthew Kingsley was six feet two and near two hundred pounds of muscle and masculinity. The civilized veneer of expensive suits and polite manners only made him more lethal.

He probably did.

Scrubbing another plate with grim energy, Kim tried for a little objectivity. What Matthew Kingsley did with his women and how he looked at them was none of her business. Nor was the degree of their luck. Their good fortune could probably be measured by the fact that they survived an encounter with him at all. Because Matt, no matter how hard he tried to look the part, was not a domesticated animal.

Kim ignored the wistful tug deep in her belly. Those women of his, like Matt, were probably born and bred in the city, wearing sophistication like a mantle. She was no match for them. All of them, including Matt, would seem like alien creatures in Posy Creek. They wouldn't fit in at all. And unlike her they'd also be bored silly in less than a day. Most visitors were.

She would be wise to remember that, she told herself firmly, because Matt's gray eyes were sending some pretty basic messages in her direction. If she had the horse sense most people credited her with, she'd steer a wide course around the owner of Kingsley Towers. He was definitely out of her league. In spite of her big-city job and trendy apartment, she knew exactly what she was—a small town girl with about as much sophistication as a turnip.

Matt nudged her gently with his elbow. "Have I put you to sleep already?"

"Don't be silly." She handed him a crystal goblet. "I'm listening. Three generations, right?" She gave him a brilliant smile.

His gaze narrowed. "Right. My grandfather was a hotelman, my father was a hotelman and I'm a—"

"Hotelman. It obviously runs in the blood."

"Or we've fallen into a very comfortable rut."

"I don't believe that for a minute," she said briskly, wringing out the sponge and watching the soapy water race down the drain. "It's obvious that you love what you're doing. The hotel reflects your lavish care as much as this house shows off the Trents' efforts. Are you done? Good. I want to show you my place."

Leading him up the curving stairway, she offered her final comment on the subject and tossed in a bit of advice for good measure. "I hope you're not thinking of changing your line of work. You're too good at what you do. You're obviously in your element here."

Flinging open her apartment door, Kim waved him in. "What do you think?" She gave her small kingdom a look that patted it on its head. "Is it great or is it great?"

Kim's enthusiasm was justified, Matt decided, surveying the spacious room. It was better than great. An elusive fragrance, floral but spicy, tugged at his senses. Miniblinds and lace curtains encouraged light to spill through the large windows onto the white wicker furniture and gleaming wooden floors. Bright cushions, an oriental rug and squads of potted plants added dramatic splashes of color. It was feminine without being fussy. It was like Kim, warm and welcoming.

Without waiting for an answer Kim led him through the large living room to a combined kitchen and dining area. "Look at this." She waved her hand at rounded walls, more large windows and more greenery. "It's the turret room. Oh, I forgot." She took him back into the other room and swung open a small glass door. "I have my own porch."

Matt poked his head out. She did indeed. It was about half the size of an elevator, brimming with more pots of green things. He met her expectant gaze. "You like flowers."

Kim grinned at the neutral tone. She was still savoring the look of pleasure that had crossed his face when he'd entered the room. "Think I've overdone it?" She took a swift look around, satisfied with what she saw. "It isn't as bad as it seems if you eliminate all the herbs I use for cooking. Besides, green is a very soothing color."

Matt gazed down at a large shallow bowl. It almost covered the top of her small television and seemed to be full of wood shavings and old flower petals. "What's this?"

"What?" Kim craned her neck to see where he was pointing. "Oh, that. Stir it with your finger."

He slanted a look at her. "That's an answer?"

"Stir," she ordered, standing beside him.

He stirred, sniffed at the delicate spicy fragrance that drifted up. "Nice." He stirred again, intrigued. "What is it?"

"Potpourri."

"What does it do?"

Kim grinned. She could practically hear his logical mind ticking away, trying to find a nice, utilitarian reason for having the stuff around. "It just sits there and smells good."

"Hmm." He gave the petals another nudge. "There's cinnamon in it."

She nodded. "Among other things. It's my own blend. I don't like things too sweet."

He had already figured that out. Unexpectedly, hunger raced through Matt with an intensity that stunned him, a need for a not-too-sweet woman with laughing eyes.

Waving him toward the largest chair and settling into one nearby, she said, "This is it, aside from the bedroom and the bath. You've had the whole twenty-five-cent tour."

His gaze moved slowly around the room again.

"What's the matter?"

"Nothing. I'm just wondering what it looked like before you moved in."

"Bare," she said succinctly, a bit surprised by the question. She hadn't pegged him as a man interested in the intricacies of interior decorating. "Jock had just painted the place, and Margo was planning to start from scratch with both apartments. When she asked me if I had any ideas, I described this." Her gesture encompassed the room. "She asked me if I wanted to do it, gave me a budget and told me to have at it while she concentrated on the other one." She lifted her shoulders in a small shrug. "So I had the pleasure of spending someone else's money and the satisfaction of getting what I wanted."

"You're good," he said abruptly.

Kim leaned back in her chair with a thoughtful expression. "What are we talking about?" she finally asked.

Matt smiled. A perceptive lady. "Your cooking, primarily." He looked around the room again. "But this is nice, too."

"Thank you. On both counts. Good enough?"

"Possibly," Matt said cautiously. He was a fool to encourage her. Excitement was already blazing in her eyes. More than likely she was already thinking of wallpaper watches and paint samples. He swore softly. He should have followed his instincts and called her, said a flat no and eliminated once and for all the complication of the restaurant between them.

"Do I hear a 'but' hanging in the air?" Kim asked.

His frowning gaze pinned her to the chair. "Yes, you do. I don't think you're experienced or hard-nosed enough to run the restaurant."

Kim took a deep breath. Well, there was honesty with a vengeance! And more of his bottom-line approach. Thank God. At least now she knew what she was up against. "What do I have to do to convince you?" she asked baldly.

"I don't know if you can."

"Then why aren't you just telling me no?"

"I was going to do exactly that, but now I've tasted your cooking."

"So what *are* you telling me?"

Matt flowed to his feet and reached for his jacket. "That you've got a week to draw up a detailed plan," he snapped, opening her door and starting down the stairs. "I want to know how you visualize the interior and layout of the tables. I want a complete description of menus and a cost analysis on equipment and personnel. And I want a damn good reason for not serving beef!"

"That's it?" she asked faintly, trotting down the stairs behind him.

"It's just the beginning." He stood in the open door way, his big frame outlined by the streetlight behind him "Stop in my office tomorrow morning and pick up the specifics from my secretary. Oh, and one more thing."

She blinked wary eyes. "What?"

Matt raised his hand and brushed the tender curve of her jaw with his thumb. "Thanks for a great dinner."

He turned and loped down the stairs before she could gather her wits. Now the ball was in her court. She had a week. If she came up with a good package, she had a restaurant. If not, she still had a job. Either way he had her. He also had the answer to his question. The name of that special woman *was* Kim Cassidy.

Three

"Calm down, Kim." Jock reached out to pat her on the shoulder as she paced by him in the entry hall. "You're going to wear a path in the new carpet."

"Stop making noises like a landlord," she told him absently, stopping at the front door to peer through the oval glass inset. "He's going to be here in ten minutes."

"With any luck he'll be early and put you out of your misery."

"Bite your tongue." She turned to face him, her eyes wide with sudden doubt. "What if I forgot something?"

"You didn't."

"Something vital, obvious." She poked at the worry with morbid conviction. "Like a salary schedule or kitchen inventory."

"Did you?"

"Well, no. At least not those things. But—"

Jock interrupted her firmly. "The only thing you forgot to do was sleep."

"Oh, that." Kim waved an impatient hand. "I can always sleep."

"If you haven't forgotten how."

Taking another peek out the window, she murmured, "Come on, Jock, it's only been a week."

"Only?"

Kim smiled at his stunned tone. He had a point. It had been a miserable, hellish week that had been far too short. Seven days—none of which had been long enough—crammed with her regular hours at the hotel plus overtime, followed by even longer hours of work at home, and a few hastily devoured meals in between that Margo had brought up and insisted she eat. And, yes, far too little sleep.

The project had not actually been that difficult; the worst part had been the time element. Under the best of conditions, compiling data and estimating and projecting costs were tedious chores; against an audibly ticking clock, they became loaded with stress. Nor had it helped to have Margo and Jock dropping in at all hours, offering their help. They had hovered and fretted, muttering their concerns about her health, endurance and sanity.

But she had done it. The report was finished. Finally. And now that it was, she could admit that she'd had serious doubts the morning after Matt's visit. His secretary had handed her a file that was nearly an inch thick, saying it was the same material that had been requested of Henri. The contents, sample forms and requests for specific information, had proved to be as intimidating as they were numerous.

"I still can't figure out how Henri ever managed to turn in a document like this," she told Jock, checking the sidewalk again.

"Why? He a little slow?"

Kim shook her head, brushing her hair behind her shoulders. "On the contrary, he's a volatile man, almost hyper. Wildly impatient with finicky details. I just can't see him sitting still long enough to compile all that information, much less put it in some presentable form."

"Which you did." Jock clearly had no interest in the Frenchman. "It looked pretty slick, kiddo."

"Yeah." Kim gave a moody nod. "But things like this are always iffy the first time around. You never know what a boss wants. If you guess wrong, you've blown it—it's too late.

"How did he expect me to get it ready in a week?" she burst out, whirling to face the older man. "It was practically impossible!" Her eyes sparkled with sudden temper. "I bet he was gambling that I *couldn't* do it, that it would be an easy way out for him. If I didn't make it, I couldn't even be considered. I'll bet he gave Henri a month. Maybe two," she added darkly. "On top of that, why did Matt insist on coming here today?"

"Matt? When did he stop being Mr. Kingsley?"

"Don't hassle me," she ordered, turning to take another quick peek out the window. "Why would he want to come here?"

Jock lifted his shoulders in a small shrug. "Who knows? Maybe he fell in love with the house. Does it matter? He can read the damned thing here as well as he can in his office."

"Yes, it matters," she said, biting off the words. "It's not . . . businesslike."

"I don't see the problem." He joined her at the window and peered over her shoulder.

"*Men.*" She gave him a disgusted glance. "It's a tactical problem. I don't know what to wear."

He took in her slim, dark brown dress, his gaze lingering on the crisp white collar. "You look wonderful. Beautiful." His comforting smile died when she scowled at him.

"I don't want to look beautiful. I want to look appropriate. I don't know if he's going to show up in one of those killer suits or . . . or jeans. I want to meet him on an equal footing." When he didn't try to hide his puzzlement she said, "I don't want to be overdressed." Or underdressed. One was as bad as the other.

"Killer suit?"

Ignoring the question, Kim pressed a hand to her diaphragm. "I think I'm hyperventilating."

"No you're not," Jock told her, easing his skinny backside into a small chair. "You're just nervous."

"Really?" She slid another disgusted look at him. "Is that my problem? Thank you, Dr. Trent."

"You gotta lighten up, kiddo, or you're going to blow the whole thing. Nerves will do you in long before your report will." His gray brows waggled, demanding her attention. "Look at it this way. What's the worst thing that could happen? Give me your top-of-the-line nightmare."

"I don't get the restaurant," she said promptly.

"And what happens if you don't? You gonna be out on the street, starving, wallowing in the gutter?" He didn't wait for an answer. "No. You'd still have a damn good job, one that you were thrilled to get in the first place. So what's the big deal here?"

"The big deal is that I want the restaurant," she said stubbornly.

"Why?"

It was an excellent question. One that Kim had asked herself repeatedly while she'd hibernated in her apartment working on the report. It was the reason she'd moved from Posy Creek. It was the chance of a lifetime, and an opportunity that compensated—a bit—for the occasional and wrenching loneliness. "It's very…important to me," she told him just as Matt eased his Mercedes to the curb.

She stiffened when he got out of the car. "Oh my God, look at him! He *has* got jeans on. Damn the man! I might've known he'd do something like this." She grabbed Jock's hand and tugged until he stood up. "You've got to stall him. Give him four minutes—no, three will be fine. Just keep him down here."

"What's all the excitement?" Margo asked as Kim raced up the stairs.

"He's wearing jeans," Jock said dryly. "What's a killer suit?"

Margo was too busy staring out of the window to answer. She watched Matt cross the sidewalk and open the gate, a frown carving two vertical lines between her brows. When she caught a glimpse of his expression she muttered, "Uh-oh," and turned to her husband. "Jock, that man has a lot more on his mind than a business report. And he doesn't look like any boss *I* ever had. If Kim was our daughter, you know what I'd be doing right now?"

He grinned. "I have an idea."

"You bet your sweet patootie you do. I'd be right on her tail, locking her in and him out."

Kim paused halfway down the stairs, smiling at the trio when they looked up. Her white long-sleeved blouse was tucked neatly into the waist of pleated, black linen slacks. One hand skimmed the banister while the other absently traced the gold chains glimmering at her neck. She didn't look like she had spent the past three minutes cursing men in general and Matt in particular while throwing one set of clothes in the closet and climbing into another.

"I see you've met Jock and Margo," she said smoothly, sliding a grateful glance toward her landlady.

Matt nodded, his unblinking gaze traveling from the dark fire of her hair down to her stylish heels. When it moved back up, gray eyes tangled with green for a few charged seconds. Matt's concentrated laser-beam regard was almost as physical as a touch, and her body was reacting as if it had been stroked. And he knew it. Darn the man. The satisfaction on his face made her fingers itch to throw something. Preferably something heavy. At him.

He was taking his own sweet time watching her, and he was making no secret of the fact that he liked what he saw. If that untethered glance was an example of not mixing business and pleasure, she didn't want to be around the day Matt tossed his scruples aside.

Jock intercepted the look and cleared his throat. "Kim, if you need—"

"Anything at all, help yourself," Margo finished smoothly, nudging him with her elbow. "We're going for a walk around the neighborhood."

Jock gave Matt a straight look. "But we won't be long."

"It's the flowers," Kim explained to Matt, coming to a halt on the bottom stair. "Everyone's out making sure that their neighbors haven't outdone them this year."

"Not true," Margo protested, looking to Jock for support. When he just shrugged and continued staring at Matt she added spiritedly, "We just like to... appreciate each other's efforts."

Matt took his eyes off Kim long enough to comment. "The whole street is lovely, but I didn't see one garden that compares with yours."

Margo smiled her appreciation. "We can thank Kim for that. She persuaded us to add a lot of native plants, ones that don't require a lot of watering. It's prettier this year than it's ever been."

"If we're going, we'd better get started," Jock said, walking over to the small closet and reaching for the sweaters that San Franciscans always kept handy. "These two have a lot of business to cover," he reminded his wife, giving Matt another level glance. "Going through that report will take a while."

After they said their goodbyes and started out the door, Matt turned to Kim. "You finished it?"

"Finished?" She looked mildly surprised. "Of course, I did. After all, you gave me a whole week."

The slamming door cut off Jock's strangled snort.

Matt stared at the door thoughtfully then turned back to Kim. "Bad wheeze he's got there," he said dryly.

"Probably an allergy," she told him without a blink, leading the way back to her apartment. "Late spring is bad for pollens."

"Yeah." Matt spoke absently, staying right where he was, the corners of his mouth turning up in a half smile. Kim in slacks, walking up stairs, was worth a bit of appreciation. The subtle sway of her hips was pure, basic woman. He decided that Kim walking up stairs in anything—or nothing—would be equally as tempting.

Nice, he reflected. Very nice. Too nice. Too distracting for a man who was supposed to be tending to business. He swore softly, dealing with an unexpected but wholly male response.

"What are you doing down there?"

Kim was standing at the top of the landing looking down, a puzzled frown drawing her brows together. "We've got work to do," she reminded him.

"Right." He grinned. He couldn't help it. She looked like a slightly exasperated teacher rounding up a recalcitrant student. A very sexy teacher.

He took the stairs three at a time and followed her into the living room, taking a quick look around. Pleasure surged through him. Nothing had changed; it was like walking from barren winter into spring. The plants, lace curtains, white walls and vivid splashes of color were as welcoming as he remembered. He sniffed appreciatively. The twigs were still working, too. Several open magazines, a newspaper folded back to the crossword puzzle and a deep rose afghan draped over an arm of the wicker couch gave the room a cozy, lived-in look.

He prowled around the large room, touching the leaves of a bright green plant, stopping to look at books that ranged from Dorothy Sayers and Gibran to the latest thrillers. Circling the room, he silently acknowledged why he had insisted on coming to her place. It had the same effect on him that the picture in his office did, only more powerful because he could walk right into it and absorb the serenity.

Applying the word serenity to anything associated with Kim should have been a contradiction in terms, he reflected, but it wasn't. Although she was a lady who ran on adrenaline she had created a restful home, a retreat where she could recharge her batteries. He had felt the pull last week and now it was working its charm on him again. The tension tying his neck and shoulders into knots had already disappeared.

"Here." Kim handed him a thick folder. "This is for you with my compliments. Do you want to sit over there?" She pointed to a small desk by a corner window, the surface of which was partially concealed by a computer. "Or the table? Your only other choice is the couch."

"Here." He sat on the couch, wondering how he was supposed to keep his mind on business when she was already jumping in with both feet, bypassing polite chitchat, taking things into her soft little hands and pushing them where she wanted them to go.

Hunger, hot and heavy, swept over him. Someday, he promised himself, she was going to take *him* in those little hands, and he knew exactly where they would end up. In bed. Hers or his, it didn't matter.

But not now. Now was for business, and for the first time since Kim had breezed into his office and dazzled him with a smile Matt found himself seriously considering her for the job, hoping she had done a passable job of the report.

Kim placed a notepad and pencil on the small coffee table near him. "Do you want something to drink? No? If you change your mind, let me know. I'll be in the dining room."

She waited until he opened the report, then turned away. She had already decided that she wouldn't stay with him, her heart in her throat, watching him read each page. She wasn't into masochism. Instead she sat down at the table, reached for a deck of cards and quietly dealt out a hand of solitaire.

Red six on the black seven.

Kim looked at her watch. The only sounds that had broken the silence in the apartment for the past hour had been those of Matt turning pages and the snap of cards hitting the table. The very least he could do is say something every now and then, let her know that he was still alive.

And impressed.

And planning to offer her the restaurant.

But businessmen didn't make encouraging noises, she reminded herself. They kept their faces blank and their mouths shut. It was a strategy she had never understood. After all, what was so bad about saying what was on your mind? She did it all the time; it cleared the air, and people knew exactly where they stood.

Kim stared at the rows of cards. Of course, she reflected wryly, that might be why Matt owned two hotels and she was just a cook. Sighing, she gathered the cards and shuffled them.

Black jack on the red queen.

If she got it, it would be an omen, Kim decided. She wasn't superstitious, but at this point she was taking whatever she could get. She needed a challenge. "Yes" would mean dig in and give it all she had. "No" would mean what? Go back to Posy Creek? Keep her job?

Kim glared at her watch. Two hours. What was he doing in there? Reading the darned thing letter by letter? At least the pages were still being turned, so she knew he wasn't asleep.

She had done a good job. Whether or not he liked it, she was proud of what she had given him. She also had a strong hunch that he was in for a surprise—at least if his alternately amused and predatory glances were an indication of how he had sized her up.

Yes, she was impulsive, she couldn't deny that. But she also had a good head for business. She might not have a poker face, but there was nothing wrong with her brain. Now the information was all there in his big hands, and it was a good, solid proposal. Looking at it strictly from a business point of view, he couldn't fault her on a thing. Of course subjectively he could hate the whole concept.

Ah well, he either liked it or he didn't. If he did, one problem was solved, but another might rear its head. A big one.

The way she reacted to Matt Kingsley was definitely not professional. For a woman who was supposed to be concentrating single-mindedly on her career, she was far too aware of him. How was she supposed to concentrate on developing a business when he was around? Everything about him was distracting: the way he loomed over her, his big beautiful hands, the essence of pure primitive male that gleamed in his eyes. He even had great buns.

Sighing, she shuffled the cards and dealt them out again.

"Do you cheat?"

Kim jumped and clutched the slick cards to keep them from sliding across the table. "A bell around your ankle might not be a bad idea," she observed calmly, gathering up the cards.

"Do you?" He dropped into the chair across from her.

"Cheat?" She shook her head. "Not even myself. Especially not myself. That would be the first crack in the dike, or so my aunts always told me. If I did cheat, I'd end up on some dark, doomed path in life. No, the guidelines they passed on to me were simple enough: Don't take advantage of people; don't try to change them; always keep your promises and always pay your debts." Her smile was soft with memories. "One of their biggest satisfactions in life is to get a receipt marked paid in full. I have to admit, I feel the same way."

She got up, poured the coffee she had brewed earlier and set the cup and saucer before him saying lightly, "I've done it again, haven't I? You ask a simple question and get a rundown on the moral guidelines of my youth. I'm going to have to do something about that."

"Not on my account."

The quiet words brought her eyes up in a rush. After examining his expressionless face for several seconds she finally said, "Tell me in words of one syllable, Matt. Don't be cryptic and make me guess, because I'd probably jump to the wrong conclusion and that would be embarrassing for both of us. Have I got it or not?"

"Yes. With certain conditions."

Kim's eyes were brilliant with triumph. "I knew it! That is, I knew you'd either love it or hate it. Tell me what you like. No, tell me what you don't like. No, tell me if you want anything changed." Lifting her cup in a toasting gesture, she said, "But first, let's celebrate. It should be champagne, but we'll have to make do with what we have. To us," she said, swinging her cup closer to him and waiting. "We're going to make wonderful partners."

Partners? Matt was speechless. She didn't waste any time. Four words from him and she'd already promoted herself from chef to a full partnership in two hotels.

His large hand covered her smaller one and forced the cup back to the saucer. "I think you're right," he said grimly. "Basic words are what we need here. Lady, I own and run two hotels and you are not my partner."

Kim retrieved her hand and waved it in the air, stopping him. "I didn't mean *partner* partner." Her earnest explanation was spoiled by the ripple of laughter in her voice. "I meant in the larger scheme of things, working together."

Matt stared at her. In the larger scheme of things, she would probably drive him crazy. But right now that didn't sound as bad as it might have last week. In fact, Matt decided, absorbing the pure gold prisms of excitement in her eyes, it didn't sound bad at all. As long as she went crazy with him. But first he had to nail down the stipulations or she'd be turning the restaurant into a three-ring circus.

No, he wasn't being fair; she wouldn't do that. After reading her very comprehensive report, he knew with certainty that in her hands the restaurant would be safe. They would be innovative hands to be sure, but capable and safe ones nonetheless. No, she might drive him to distraction, but she had too much savvy to jeopardize a business.

He tapped the thick file that she had given him. "This is good. Very good."

Kim pursed her lips. "Surprised you, huh?"

"Yes, you did."

"I minored in business in college," she admitted. The words seemed more of an apology than an explanation.

"I won't tell anyone," he promised with a swift grin. "So what are the conditions?"

Matt sighed. As usual she was not just passing go, she was waiting at the bottom line. "Stipulations," he corrected.

"Whatever." She waited impatiently.

"First, I want the place to look like your apartment."

Kim looked around. She was astonished. Speechless. Matt decided to savor the silence. It probably wouldn't happen again for a long time. Besides, it gave him a chance to watch the emotions flickering on her expressive face.

He was right. It didn't last long.

"Like *this*?" she asked in disbelief. "Why? There's nothing special about it. In fact, it's exactly the way my house in Posy Creek looks. It's not precisely what I had in mind," she began carefully. "Let me tell you a little bit more about what I—"

"Like this," he said firmly. "Or not at all."

Kim eyed him doubtfully, then shook her head. "Okay. If that's what you want." Her tone indicated that she was humoring him.

"That's exactly what I want." He leaned back, relaxing. It was going to be easier than he'd thought, he reflected. She was impulsive and could talk the hind leg off a donkey, but she was also reasonable. "Now, about the menus."

Kim's eyes narrowed.

"I like the sample you designed. I also like the appetizers, salads and desserts you listed. The weak spot is the entrées. We need more specifics. What are your specialities?"

Kim shook her head.

"What does that mean? You don't have any specialities?"

"More than I can count," she said coolly. "But they don't belong on a menu, they belong in the kitchen where the work is being done. What good does it do to list salmon on the menu if you can't buy any? What good does it do to list trout if the catch is poor? I'm very finicky about what comes into my kitchen, and I won't have it brought in just because it's listed on the menu."

She leaned forward, talking fast. "My idea is to list all of the fish as the chef's specialty or catch of the day or whatever fancy name we want to call it. That way we can buy the best and be proud of what we serve. When the customers come in, the waiters will tell them what's on the menu. You know," she pointed out, "it's psychologically valid, too. The waiters are more involved and the customers feel more knowledgeable and discriminating."

There was an obstinate look in her green eyes as she continued. "I won't be put in the position of having to apologize for what I serve."

Matt eyed her thoughtfully. It could work. San Franciscans prided themselves on their adaptability. They also sought out the new and different. Yes, it could work.

"All right," he conceded. "But the same argument doesn't hold true for the chicken. Why aren't you listing those dishes?"

"I want room to be creative," she said stubbornly. "A menu is too restricting."

"Hold one entrée open for creativity. Call it whatever you want. List the others." His tone was final. "Also, I want to try every meal, and I have final menu approval."

"*What?*"

"I told Henri the same thing," he said blandly.

"And what did Henri tell you?"

"He was too smart to even try objecting. He invited me to dinner instead."

Kim lowered her lashes just in case her satisfaction was showing. He had already conceded far more than she had expected. Professor Norton would have been proud of her. Stunned was more like it, she amended after a moment's thought. The instructor had washed his hands of her after she had turned a negotiating workshop into near chaos, telling her to concentrate on her cooking and leave the business to the hardball players.

She remembered explaining that she understood the concepts; her only problem was the actual confrontation, she talked too much. His solution had been for her to substitute written assignments for class arguments. She had gotten very good at making outrageous demands on paper. And that was exactly what she had done with Matt. At the very most she had expected one free slot with the fish and none with the chicken, but what she'd been given was exactly what she had wanted.

She made a mental note to call her old teacher and let him know that one of his business strategies had been successful. It was the least she could do for the poor man.

Matt cleared his throat. "Well?"

"Okay," she agreed reluctantly, getting into the spirit of things. "Dinner."

"Each and every meal," he reminded her. "Dinners." He emphasized the plural, satisfaction gleaming in his eyes.

She just might have been missing out on a good thing all these years, Kim reflected, watching Matt like a hawk through her lashes. He was undeniably pleased. He had just won a series of home-cooked meals, yet she hadn't lost a thing, since creating a memorable meal was high on her own list of priorities. This negotiating technique definitely merited some more thinking, she decided. Along with looking and leaping.

She nodded again. "Dinners."

"Now, about the beef."

The telephone rang, giving Kim a reprieve. "We'll talk about it," she promised, moving over to the bar and picking up the receiver.

"You bet we will," he muttered.

"Uncle Theo! How are you? And the aunts, are they fine, too? Good. What's up?"

How would it feel to have someone light up like that when she heard your voice? Matt wondered. No, not someone. Kim. Trying to look as if he wasn't listening, he got up and wandered over to the bookshelves by the kitchen window. It was no surprise to find that they were filled with cookbooks. The selection, he noted, again without surprise, was as eclectic as the collection in the other room.

"Where are you going this time?" Kim asked, perching on one of the stools and reaching for a pencil. "Wait a minute, let me get some paper. Okay, New York on the fourteenth, then Boston, Tampa, Chicago, Saint Louis, Oklahoma City."

She listened to a lengthy explanation. "By that time you'll need a break," she agreed. "Then on to Las Vegas, Seattle and Portland. You're going to have your hands full. Yes, of course. You know I will. If I'm lucky, I'll be able to wangle a few days up there with them. Love you. Enjoy and take care. Bye."

She cradled the receiver and turned to Matt. "That was my uncle. Great-uncle, actually. He and my aunts were my grandmother's brother and sisters. He's going on a trip."

"Sounds like quite an itinerary for such an old man." Matt leaned a shoulder against the wall and waited for the rest. He was getting used to Kim dotting and crossing all the verbal *i*'s and *t*'s.

"Uncle Theo has more energy than a troop of Boy Scouts. He's also one of the country's foremost experts on medicinal herbs, and several times a year he goes on lecture tours."

"And he's getting ready to go on one now?"

She nodded. "In a few days. He always calls me so I can keep in touch with the aunts."

"Do you need some time off to stay with them?"

She shook her head emphatically, causing her dark hair to slide forward over her breasts. "I wouldn't dare. They're as spry and independent as Uncle Theo, and they'd get upset if they thought I was baby-sitting. No, the most I can do is call more often and try to go up for a weekend."

She slid off the stool and went back to the table, her mind returning to the troublesome topic of beef. He'd undoubtedly want to talk about it now.

"You can arrange more time than that if you need to," Matt told her. "I was going to suggest you stay on at the Pyramid Room for a couple of days until they can replace you, and then concentrate on setting up the new restaurant."

Her level look would have flattened a lesser man. "You think I can be replaced in two days? Thank you very much. Maybe I can help you find my successor. I'll be happy to stop at a couple of fast-food joints in the morning and see if any of the fry cooks are available."

"That's not what I meant and you know it." Matt knew better than to grin at the frosty comment. She looked mad enough to nail him to the wall with a carving knife. It was obvious that while Kim might take a lot of things lightly, her cooking ability wasn't one of them.

"If no one's available, they'll just have to survive without you," he said bluntly. "Because we have a lot to do and not much time to do it in."

Her brows rose. "We?"

"We. I'm going to be right beside you every step of the way."

"Why?"

"It's the way I always work," he lied. "It's my hotel, my privilege to sit in on a new project."

Her eyes narrowed. "Would you have done it with Henri?"

"Yes." For an hour or two.

"And who has the final vote when a decision is called for?" she asked suspiciously.

"For now, I do."

"And what kind of a manager will that make me?" she demanded, her eyes stormy. "No one will take me seriously. Matt, you can't give someone a title and hold back the authority that goes with it. It's a no-win situation."

He sighed in exasperation. Did she think he didn't know that? "Give me credit for a little subtlety, will you? When we set up meetings with the people you need to know, it will merely serve as an opportunity to introduce you to contacts." And give those with an ounce of sense the assurance that he was backing her. "Before we walk into a situation, we'll make sure that we're on the same wavelength. But when we actually get there, you'll be on your own."

"Oh."

Surprise flickered in her eyes as she digested his statement, and some of the starch went out of her shoulders, but he saw the exact moment she realized that some of those preliminary discussions were going to be humdingers. With a blink of her long lashes she put that issue aside and geared up for the next one.

"Matt," she began with determination, "about the beef. Statistics show that people are eating less of it than they ever have, and I want to capitalize on that fact. The people who will make up our clientele are the type who are concerned about the fat content in food—at least most of them are," she added honestly. "They're not ordering heavy beef meals. Those who are can get them anywhere in the city."

Her eyes were fired with enthusiasm. "I want to give them choices that they've never had before. I want—"

"Okay."

"—to show them that . . ." She stopped, eyeing him uncertainly. "What did you say?"

He sighed. He seemed to be doing a lot of sighing these days. "Okay. You've made your point. We'll stick to chicken and fish. For now. If it doesn't work, we'll talk about it again later."

"Right." She lifted her cup. "Now can we toast our new venture?"

He touched the edge of his cup to hers and took a sip. "Why do I get the feeling that there are tail feathers all around your sweet little mouth?"

Kim's laugh was a soft teasing sound. "You have a very active imagination, Mr. Kingsley."

"No." He shook his head deliberately. "What I have is a strong urge to love you until you melt all over me."

Four

"Matt!" Kim jumped to her feet, caught off guard.

Moving until he stood in front of her, he said, "You can't be that surprised."

"Well...I am." Not so much at what he said; she had felt it coming, had known it would happen sooner or later. But, she reflected, backing up until her bottom nudged the edge of the table, she had figured on it happening later. Much later. Kim frowned at the miscalculation. Normally her sense of timing was better. Since Matt had a corporate image to consider, it had seemed only logical that he would at least wait until their business together was settled.

"Why?" His single word was smooth as butter and more of a challenge than she wanted to face.

Kim's eyes widened when he moved closer, stopping just before they touched. Heat radiated from his big body and she tried to edge back another inch or two. The table didn't budge, leaving her right where she was—a heat wave away from him. Damn the man, she wasn't ready for this!

"I'm entitled to surprise," she stalled, reaching behind her for leverage and sliding up to perch on the table. "After all, you, uh, own two hotels. I'm just a cook in one of them."

"What I have and where you work doesn't have a thing to do with this." Nudging her knees apart, Matt moved between her legs. Ignoring her gasp, he filled his hands with her dark hair, making a small sound of pleasure deep in his throat when the silky stuff slid through his fingers. "It's amazing how you go from a hotshot chef to 'just a cook' when the mood strikes you," he murmured, releasing her hair and watching it tumble down and settle over her breasts. "But spare me the Cinderella routine. I can't picture you as a victim." A smile tugged at his lips.

She should have been reassured by the amusement warming Matt's voice and the remnant of pleasure lingering in his smoky eyes. And she might have been if she hadn't glimpsed the determination that was written all over his face. Kim took a shaky breath. With Matt's legs pressed against her thighs and his big hands sliding down her back to her bottom, every square inch of her body seemed to be touching his.

When Matt moved, he did it with the overpowering inevitability of an avalanche, she reflected. She should have expected it. *Would* have expected it if she hadn't been so preoccupied.

"Who we are or what we have has nothing to do with this," he repeated. His hands moved back to her shoulders and he drew her nearer, until the tips of her breasts touched his hard chest. Fire shot through his body with a pleasure that was close to pain. When Kim shuddered and took a quick breath, he knew she felt it too. Wrapping his arms around her and tugging her even closer, he said, "I knew it the minute you walked into my office, and if you'll be honest, you'll admit that you did, too."

"I'm always honest," she said indignantly, her voice muffled against his knit shirt.

"So tell me," he demanded. "Did you?"

"I'm probably getting lipstick all over you," she evaded, wiggling until she realized that it was useless. Matt's hands were gentle, but he wasn't about to let her go.

"I'll survive." One large hand cupped her head, his fingers closing around her hair. When she looked up he said again, "Did you?"

"Matt," she wailed softly, "I don't want this kind of complication in my life."

"Did you?"

It was worse than water dripping on a stone. Water didn't wrap itself around the rock, sharing heat and a heartbeat with it. Water didn't have a voice that reverberated, sending blood singing dizzily through the poor shattered stone. Water didn't have a body hard with primitive male hunger. Water wasn't Matthew Kingsley.

"Kim." It wasn't a question. Gentle as it was, it was a command.

"All right," she said grudgingly. "Yes, I did. But I told myself that it was the wrong time and the wrong place and the wrong people."

"Two out of three isn't bad." His smile drove her crazy.

"*And* I told myself to forget it."

"That was quite a conversation you had."

Recklessly she asked, "What do you mean, 'two out of three'?"

His breath touched her cheek. "An office is an awkward place to make love—too many interruptions." He watched in interest as her eyes narrowed, sending a mute promise of retaliation. He could hardly wait.

"And the timing was definitely wrong. We were there on business, and if things were going to work out we had to wait."

"Wait?"

He nodded, his lips moving closer to her mouth. "Um, until our business was settled."

"Matt." She squirmed again, with no more success this time than she'd had the last. "I hate to be the one to tell you this, but our business is just beginning. We've got the same reasons against doing this now that we had a week ago." She slid her hands to his chest and pushed. He was just like the table, he didn't budge.

Matt's lips touched the corner of her mouth. "That's not the way I see it. Last week a restaurant stood between us. Now it doesn't."

"Is that why I have it?" Ice edged the soft words, and her hands pressed against his biceps.

"No." He nodded to the thick folder on the table. "That's why you have it, and no other reason." Her nails stopped digging into his skin and he let out a long slow breath. "I stayed away from you for a week, until it was settled. I knew it would be over tonight, one way or another."

"But it *isn't*." Kim stared straight ahead at his shirt. She couldn't think. He was too hot, too big, too unnerving.

She wasn't afraid of Matt. She knew that if she flat out told him to let her go, he would. The major problem with that was that he felt good. Too good. And she couldn't quite get the words out. Three short syllables—"let me go"—and she couldn't say them. But she would...in a minute or two.

The trouble with temptation, she reflected hazily, was that it was so *tempting*. And that's exactly what Matthew Kingsley was. Over six feet two of forbidden fruit. She should be telling him exactly what he could do with his cockamamy ideas. And she would. In a while.

She should put some starch in her spine and move away from his warmth. And she would. Soon.

Kim sat up straighter. Now was the time, she told herself firmly. Now, before all hope of salvaging the evening, and the restaurant, was gone. Making her voice as brisk as she could, she said, "You're not making any sense. You just told me that we're going to be working together. You also told me that you don't mix business with pleasure."

"I'm willing to make you an exception."

"Do I have a say in this?" she asked politely. "If I do—"

Matt bent his head, stopping an inch away from her mouth, his warm breath merging with hers. Softly, so softly, he stopped her, brushing his lips over hers, touching the corner of her mouth, her cheek, the delicate skin at the outer edge of her eye.

Kim prided herself on being a fast learner. This moment was no exception. At the touch of Matt's mouth she learned that curiosity rated right up there with practicality. A thirst for knowledge ranked every bit as high as horse sense. And right now she needed to know how it felt to kiss Matt. One kiss she promised herself. Just one. After that, once she knew, she'd be back on track. She'd tell him...whatever it was she was supposed to be telling him.

She sighed, leaning into him, using her fingertips in his hair, bringing his mouth back to hers. Her hands dug into his shoulders when he tugged her toward him, clung to them when he lifted her and turned until he was half sitting on the edge of the table.

"Come closer." His voice was urgent. "I need you closer."

And she went. Stepping into the cradle of his thighs, giving her mouth to him again, murmuring in wordless pleasure. Her fingers skimmed his face, his shoulders, down his chest, telling him more than she knew. Giving him more than she wanted.

"I want you, Kim. God, I want you so much."

The muttered words finally penetrated, finally made sense. When they did they hit her like a shock of cold water. Kim stiffened and lifted her head. Want? *Want?* Was that all it amounted to? I want, I'll take and then we'll get back to business?

"Let me go, Matt."

It seemed to take forever, but the cool determination in her voice finally reached him. His arms gradually loosened, but his big hands lingered at her waist, steadying her, then slowly let her go.

"What's the matter?" Concern roughened his voice.

Kim stepped back, smoothing her hair, taking her time until she was sure her voice was steady. "We all want things in life, Matt. Some we get and some we don't. I don't come with a management package."

Matt swore, slowly and fluently. "You think that I don't know that?"

"Suddenly I have my doubts."

Stalking over to the window, he jammed his hands in his back pockets and stared at the streetlights below. When he turned back to her, his voice was even. "I'll say this one more time. First, you're the manager of the new restaurant because of that." He nodded at the report on the table. "You convinced me that you can do the job. There are no sexual strings attached to the offer. Are you with me so far?"

Kim nodded. He was mad; he wasn't making any secret of the fact. Fine. So was she.

"Second, I place no moral or emotional restrictions on my employees. I don't give a damn who is dating, living with or married to whom as long as they do their jobs. I give myself the same leeway."

He moved a couple of steps closer. "So that brings us back to us. When we're together, the tension is so thick it could be cut with one of your fancy knives. Can you deny that?"

Kim shook her head, waiting. Her time would come.

Snagging one of the chairs, he turned it around and straddled it, draping his arms along the back. "Good. So what do we do about it?"

"You've got the floor." Kim crossed her arms, daring him with an intense look. "You tell me."

In spite of his anger, Matt almost laughed. She was just waiting for a chance to nail him to the wall. Practically begging him to come across like a macho idiot and say something about taking her to bed. The problem was, he *was* feeling like a macho idiot and that was exactly what he wanted to say. Fortunately the genes of three generations of business sharks, who also happened to be pretty fair poker players, had taught him when to bluff and when to keep his mouth shut. And how to capitalize on these skills when dealing with those who hadn't learned the lessons.

"We're going to be seeing a lot of each other in the next couple of months," he reminded her. "I suggest that we take advantage of the time and get better acquainted. See where the whole thing takes us."

Kim's eyes narrowed in suspicion. He was too offhand, too charming. "How?"

"The same way that other couples do." His broad shoulders lifted in a careless shrug. "Going out to dinner.

Whatever. It's not that complicated. I think we can manage it and still get the job done."

"I think it's a rotten idea," she said stonily. "When I work, I work. I don't have time to play games."

His brows lifted. "If I were a gambler, I'd bet that you thoroughly enjoy yourself at work."

Kim scowled. "I do."

"That's all I'm asking. Work as hard as you want but have fun while you're doing it. With me."

"And what'll you be doing?" He was up to something. She could feel it in her bouncing pulse. No smile that bland could be honest.

"I'll be declaring open season on redheaded chefs."

"I knew it!" she exploded, throwing out her arms in exasperation. "Who do you think you are, the great white hunter? Darn it, Matt, I'm serious about this. I want this restaurant to be a success, and unless you've completely lost your mind, so do you." She tapped her foot impatiently. "I've got a job cut out for me, and now is the time to work. I need to concentrate on pulling things together. I don't have time to—"

"That's fine," he said calmly. "I want it to be a success as much as you do. But you have to eat, you have to relax sometime. When you do, I want to be with you." He reached out a long arm for the folder and absently straightened the sheaf of papers, selecting his words carefully.

"We're in this for the long haul," he reminded her. "If you go at this with a damn-the-torpedoes attitude for eighteen hours a day, you'll burn out in a week."

"It's the way I work best."

"You have to pace yourself."

Kim wrinkled her nose. "Sounds deadly dull."

He shrugged. "It may not carry you on an adrenaline rush, but it gets the job done."

"I suppose. You realize that we'll probably drive each other crazy, don't you? We'll be at each other's throats in less than a day."

"I doubt if it'll go that far," he said easily, getting to his feet. "Don't bother coming down with me. I'll see myself out."

"Matt!" Kim followed him through the living room, scowling when he opened the door. "We're not through talking."

"You have two days to finish in the Pyramid Room," he reminded her, bracing his shoulder against the doorjamb, enjoying her look of frustration. "Then we're going shopping."

"For what?"

"Furniture."

"Furniture." She repeated the word as if she'd never heard it before.

He nodded. "For the restaurant. By the way, we've got to find another name for the place. Think about that."

"Oh, sure. In my spare time. What kind of furniture?"

"Like the things over there." His nod took in her cherished old English pie safe and the large pine dresser that she used to display a collection of jelly molds.

"Matt!" Kim's voice rose. "You don't just run down to the furniture store and buy these things. They're antiques. *Genuine* antiques."

She would be reasonable if it killed her, Kim told herself. Lowering her voice, she said, "I didn't buy them when I furnished the place. They belong to me. They've been in the family for years, and I brought them from Posy Creek."

Matt gave her a polite nod that said, "I hear you," and looked at his watch.

"We could spend months looking for stuff like this," she persevered. "And if we were lucky enough to find anything within a hundred miles of here, we'd pay a fortune for it."

"It's a good thing we have a fortune, isn't it?"

"But we don't have the time." She said the words slowly, emphatically, wondering if she was getting through to him at all.

Matt grinned. "Then we'll make it. Since we're changing the whole concept, I think we can give ourselves another month." He checked his watch again. "See you Thursday morning, nine sharp. I'll pick you up here. Dress comfortably, I have a feeling it'll be a long day."

Kim didn't try to stop him. It took all her control not to slam the door behind him. Leaving was the best idea he'd had all night, other than giving her the restaurant. And since he had been three jumps ahead of her all evening, he could obviously find the way back to his car without her help.

She walked over to the window, seething with bad temper and frustrated energy. This must be a classic case of winning the battle and losing the war, she realized, watching the lights of Matt's elegant car stab at the darkness. She had been outclassed and outmaneuvered from the moment he'd walked through her front door.

But she had got what she wanted.

Hadn't she?

Yes, she assured herself. Definitely. Fate and Matt Kingsley had decreed that her future lay in San Francisco. She had a restaurant! She just hadn't known that Matt would be part of the deal, and the idea took some getting used to.

"Kim?" Margo tapped on the door. "Are you still up?"

Smiling at the shameless curiosity in the older woman's voice, Kim swung the door open. "Hi."

"Jock told me not to bother you, but I couldn't wait until tomorrow. Was he impressed? Did he like it? Did you get it?"

Kim waved her to the couch. When they were both seated she said, "Yes, yes, and yes."

"I'm so proud of you." Margo gave her a swift hug. "Now, tell me all about it."

It didn't take all that long. Judicious editing shortened the story considerably. "So," Kim concluded a few minutes later, "I have a restaurant that doesn't have a name. I wrung concessions from Matt I never expected to win—and I did it all without a struggle. The opening will be delayed to give us more time, and I have a boss attached to me like a Siamese twin."

"No problem." Margo gestured airily. "You'll handle him just like that." She snapped her fingers to show how simple the whole thing would be. Growing serious, she said, "But you're not as excited as I thought you'd be. What's wrong?"

It was a good question. Hours later, trying to block out the distant sounds of traffic, Kim shifted restlessly in bed, trying to find an answer.

"What do you think of The Country Kitchen?" Kim's pencil was poised over the list she had compiled during the past two days.

Matt winced.

"No? Okay, scratch that. How about The Aerie? After all, it is going to be on the top floor."

"I don't think so."

Kim closed the notebook with an irritated snap. "I tell you what. You come up with some names for a while and let *me* say no."

"I didn't say we had to name the place today. We've got time." He signaled with his blinker and changed lanes, heading south to Saratoga.

"Not a heck of a lot." Kim flipped the pages of her organizer, checking the calendar. "Not if we're going to get an ad campaign moving."

"Relax. It'll work out. You can even put your book down and take a few minutes to look at the scenery." Matt kept his voice soothing. Despite the classy restraint of the executive-type blazer and slacks Kim wore, she was a jumble of nerves. She had been talking nonstop since she had stepped out of the house and spotted his big, shiny black 4x4.

A slight smile curving his lips, he reflected that she undoubtedly thought she looked conservative and businesslike. And appropriate. That was important to Kim. In spite of her slapdash manner, she set great store by having things in their proper order.

Maybe other women would agree with her, but any man with eyes in his head and breath in his body would know that her outfit was sexy as hell. She wouldn't be pleased. His smile grew broader at the thought. If she was so set on looking brisk and efficient, she shouldn't wear dark green clothes that turned her eyes to jade and brought out the fire in her hair. Clothes that made her shimmer with exotic energy. Clothes that turned a man's thoughts to touching and stroking.

Her dark red hair was just as tempting, caught in a casual swirl on top of her head, held up with some bit of invisible feminine magic. Wispy tendrils were already breaking loose, brushing the delicate curve of her nape.

Kim gazed out at the rolling green hills for a long moment. When she turned to him, a look of speculation on her face, Matt braced himself. That look usually meant she had decided to hit him with another innovation, one designed to chill his blood. He had a sneaking suspicion that she stayed awake nights hatching these things just to see how far she could push him.

"I had an idea last night." As usual she rushed in full tilt. "Before we open, I want the entire staff to sample the meals on the menu."

"*All* of them?"

She grinned at his stunned look. "Of course. All the staff, all the meals."

"Do you have any idea what that will cost?" he demanded.

Kim settled back in the seat, anticipation gleaming in her eyes. "To the penny. A very *pretty* penny, I might add."

"No."

"Now, Matt." She held up a calming hand, grinning. "Let's not rush into a decision that we'll regret."

"We're not—" his voice was adamant "—I am. No."

"You're in no position to make an informed judgment," she told him. "Not yet. I, on the other hand, have given it a great deal of thought."

"I don't have to be informed," he grunted. "I'm the boss."

"We'll consider it a dress rehearsal. No, don't look so horrified, I've got it all figured out. The cost of the food should be deductible."

"In which country?"

"You're not getting into the spirit of this thing. Tell your tax people to be creative. They should be able to chalk it up to education or instructional material."

He slid her a disbelieving look. She was serious. "Would you like to explain that to an auditor?"

"Sure." Her smile was easy. "No problem. Look at it this way. The people who take the orders and serve the food are our sales staff, right?"

He nodded.

"So I want them to know the texture of the food, the subtle flavors. They'll recommend a meal with a lot more knowledge and enthusiasm if they've actually tasted it."

"Let me get this straight. Every time you fix up a new recipe, they'll eat it first?"

"Don't make it sound like they're a plague of locust descending on the year's crops," she reproved. "Of course they will. That's the whole idea. They can't sell the product if they don't know what it tastes like."

"I know a lot of restauranteurs who would disagree."

She nodded in agreement. "Yeah, I know some of them, too. They're the same ones whose hired help tells a customer they haven't tried the food, but they hear it's pretty good. Aren't we lucky that the owner of Kingsley Tower is more farsighted?" Her eyes provoked him.

"Don't push your luck," he advised with a lazy grin, checking the rearview mirror and moving over to the slow lane.

Kim stood her ground, smiling at him. "A new wind is blowing through Kingsley's. After all, how many other hotel owners would drag one of their chefs to every antique store within a hundred-mile radius looking for furniture?"

Matt took a long look at her laughing face. A lot of them, he reflected. If they were male and had the same ulterior motive that he did. If they wanted to know what emotion intensified the green in her eyes, what triggered her quick temper and what would make her pliant and shiver in a man's arms. Yeah, if they had that incentive they'd go as far as they had to, as fast as they could. Especially, he reminded himself, if they'd had the intelligence to recognize her latent business skills as well.

Following the green sign above the off-ramp, he said, "Why did you pick Saratoga for our first stop?"

"Why not?" She shrugged. "It seemed like a good enough possibility. It's a settled community. Some of the families have lived in the same houses for a couple of generations. And even though it's the kind of place where people hang on to family heirlooms, antique stores do eventually get some of them."

Several hours later she climbed back in the car and eased off her shoes while Matt slid in beside her. Discreetly wiggling her toes, she said, "Nothing. Again. Apparently I was wrong. Saratoga's heirlooms *don't* end up in antique stores. At least not the kind we're looking for."

"It wasn't a total loss," he reminded her, looking down at the box he was holding. "Besides, it was only the fifth one we've been in."

Kim shot him a dark glance. Unfortunately he wasn't indulging in a little male sarcasm; he meant it.

Reaching down to massage her arch, she decided that, contrary to her previous optimistic supposition, life was really not fair. Otherwise, with all the men in the world who turned pale at the thought of a shopping expedition, why was she cursed with one who had taken to antiquing with all the zest of a miner turned loose in a mother lode?

The result had been the same in each shop. Matt had been like a kid in a candy store, opening everything openable. Poking and prodding everything that wasn't. Kim stifled a moan and flexed her toes again. He might have ruined her arches, but he had endeared himself to five store owners—and he had a growing collection of old cooking gadgets in the back seat.

"Matt, we've got to find a better system." She tapped his shoulder with her finger to get his attention. "You can't look through every old cookbook, examine every item in every store. At this rate the only thing we'll have when the restaurant opens will be knickknacks."

"Um." He propped the corner of the box on the steering wheel and looked inside. The proud satisfaction in his gaze reminded her of a father looking at his firstborn. He reached inside and held up a contraption that cored and peeled apples.

"What do you think, honey? If we ever find a pie safe like the one in your living room, this can go on the shelf."

"Very nice," she murmured absently, blinking at the endearment. Somehow, sometime between the electric kiss the other night and Matt's arrival this morning, their relationship had changed. At least, while she had spent two days assuring herself that they were both too professional to allow it to happen again, his half had changed—without so much as an interoffice memo to warn her.

When she had opened her door, ready to leave and determinedly brisk, he had dropped a quick, hard kiss on her upturned lips then hustled her outside and into his rugged 4x4 before she'd had time to protest. Since then, the underlying message beneath every look from his gray eyes, every touch, had been the same: There was no going back.

Kim's sigh was frazzled. Ignoring him hadn't helped, had done nothing to reduce the palpable tension in the car. Now settling for something she *could* handle she said, "Matt, at this rate, we're never going to finish. The idea is to walk in the store, look for furniture and leave if they don't have what we want."

"Right." He replaced the apple peeler and put the box on the back seat. "Where are we going next?"

"You're a menace," she told Matt as the waiter walked away. "I hope you don't plan to charge that last atrocity to *my* budget."

He grinned, covering her hand with his when she reached for the menu. "It's for the restaurant."

She shook her head and told her leaping pulse to settle down. "No way. You don't have the foggiest idea what it is. Even the people in the store didn't have a clue. You get to keep it until you identify it."

Matt buttered a roll and popped a piece in his mouth. "It won't go with the decor in my place."

"Tough. It looks like a leftover from a medieval torture chamber, and it definitely won't fit in with my Posy Creek look. Nope, it's all yours."

"Last chance," he offered.

"Forget it." She took a swallow of wine. Fortified, she dipped her fork in the salad. "You know what I think?"

"What?" Matt watched her sniff the fork with the delicacy of a cat, before touching it to the tip of her tongue.

Kim gave a resigned sigh. "That we're going to have a very mediocre meal. I also think that if today's progress is any indication, it's going to take a long time to find what we need for the restaurant. On top of that, I think that you look very pleased with yourself. You must really like the unidentified object you bought for such an outrageous price."

Matt took a bite of salad and chewed thoughtfully. Kim was right about the meal. It was going to need all the help the excellent wine could offer. But the satisfaction she picked up on had nothing to do with the widget and everything to do with Kim herself.

The fact that they hadn't found the furniture yet was immaterial. He would have been surprised if they had. He knew as well as Kim that pieces like her own antiques weren't easily come by. No, the purpose for the trip had been a simple one: to get Kim accustomed to being with him. And that was exactly what had happened. First she had lost the reserve she had wrapped herself in since that kiss the other night, then most of her wariness. There was still an occasional flicker of caution in her eyes, but she was back to snapping out orders. It was the first step.

"Does Saratoga remind you of Posy Creek?"

Kim considered the question while she took another bite of salad. "A little. The rural atmosphere more than anything."

"You've told me all the good things about Posy Creek. What you haven't told me is why you left."

Kim sighed. "It wasn't easy. But I was too comfortable there. If I intended to make it as a chef, I had to go. It's not exactly a gourmet's haven; most people there prefer hamburgers. And, Matt, the pace is so *slow*. Everything revolves around the seasons. You plant the crops and wait months for them to grow. Then you pick them and more months pass while you sell them. By that time you're ready to plant again. It was driving me crazy."

She poked at the trout on her plate, then smiled, her eyes brimming with enthusiasm. "And I absolutely fell in love with San Francisco. I wanted the hustle of crowds. I wanted challenge and excitement and people who appreciated my talent."

"And glamour?"

She considered that briefly, then shook her head. "No, that's not a big need in my life. It's the electric feeling of being alive every second of the day that I love. There's an energy in San Francisco that's contagious, and a good reason it's called 'The City That Knows How.' The people here know how to have fun, they live life to its fullest."

Kim reached across the table and touched his hand. Her voice gentled. "And sometimes they take a chance on a newcomer. Matt, I haven't told you how much I appreciate your trust. I want you to know that I'll never let you down like Henri did. Come hell or high water, I finish what I start. Whatever happens, I'll give you a restaurant that will make the people in this city sit up and take notice."

Five

"Uh-oh, you've pulled Shangri-la out again. You must have had a bad day yesterday."

Matt's secretary stared thoughtfully at the papers strewn across Matt's desk and finally nudged a few aside, replacing them with a brightly colored folder. "These are the latest figures from Kim."

"Thanks, Mary." He pushed his chair back and swung around to face her. "What do you mean, Shangri-la?"

"My name for your pet project."

His brows rose. "Since when?"

"Since two years ago, the day you first told me about it."

Although Mary was approaching sixty, the only indication was the silvery cap of hair that she refused to tint. She had a mind like a razor and the body and skin of a much younger woman. She dressed with the sleek confidence of a model, and she guarded his office door with the ferocity of an attack dog.

Frowning, Matt asked, "You're not coming in to tell me that you're retiring, are you?"

"Why do you keep asking me that?" She sat in the chair by his desk and eyed him in exasperation.

"We've had three retirement parties in the past two months and I'm getting nervous."

"Well, I wish you'd stop. It makes me feel old. Older," she amended with ironic humor. "Look, I've just whipped you into shape, I'd be a fool to leave now." She shook her head. "No, I'm here because I'm worried about you. You've been so quiet these past few days I thought I'd run in and do a quick pulse and temperature check."

"I'm fine." Matt looked down at the blueprint unrolled on his desk.

"I might believe that if you weren't poring over Shangri-la," Mary said dryly. "Some men handle stress and incipient burnout by losing their tempers or having affairs. You pull out these blueprints and dream."

Matt's smile was a wry admission. "How long have we been working together?"

"You know that as well as I do. Six years. And that's not counting the twenty you were around while I kept your father in line. Anyway, it's been long enough for me to know when the city is crowding you." Her brisk tone failed utterly to hide her concern.

He gave her a thoughtful stare, considering her words. "Why Shangri-la?" he asked finally.

Mary's slim shoulders lifted in a shrug. "Why not? What else would you call perfection? A gem of an executive treat," she quoted from memory, ticking off the salient points on her fingers. "A spa for stressed-out businessmen. Rustic, small and intimate. Cottages built in the hollows of perfectly formed rolling hills. Located in a paradise where the few people around are friendly and know all the good fishing spots. Have I left anything out?''

"Built and operated by?" he prompted.

"The one and only Matthew Kingsley."

"I think that about covers it. Are you telling me in your own tactful way that you think I'm never going to pull it off?"

She shook her head, returning his easy smile. "No, I think you're seeing it more clearly all the time, and I consider that inner vision an essential ingredient of success. I believe that someday, if you find the right place, it will happen."

"When I find it."

"When," she agreed, smiling again at his adamant tone.

Matt rubbed the back of his neck. "Don't even think of retiring for the next five years or so. I'd miss these little pep talks.

"As well as someone to run the office," she said dryly. "I'll be around for a while. Probably until you find Shangri-la. Once that happens, I have a feeling that you won't need me, because—" Mary looked at the blinking red light on his telephone and leaned forward to pick up the receiver. "Mr. Kingsley's office." Her voice warmed. "Hi, Kim. Yes, he's here." Silently she handed him the phone.

Matt covered the mouthpiece with his hand. "I won't need you because . . . what?"

"Because you'll more than likely take one look at Eden and decide to stay." She gave him a pat on the shoulder and walked to the door, noiselessly closing it behind her.

"Matt? Hi." Kim's voice was eager. "I was just looking at a map for tomorrow. Sutter Creek might be a possibility. They have scads of antique shops there."

Smiling at the thread of anticipation in her voice, Matt leaned back and propped his feet on the corner of the desk. It hadn't come easy, and Kim wouldn't be pleased that she was so transparent. She had argued every step of the way but had finally agreed that finding the chests and other large accessories for the restaurant was a priority. Matt had suggested three shopping expeditions a week; she had held out for one. They compromised on two—which was what Matt had wanted in the first place. Sometimes, he mused, he really outdid himself.

Tension eased out of his shoulders and neck at the lilt in her voice. He decided that the AMA was missing a good thing in Kim; she was positively therapeutic. He didn't know if it was her warmth, her enthusiasm, her open-armed approach to life or a combination of all three, but whatever she had, it was potent.

It could be bottled and sold for a fortune as an anti-depressant, he mused, listening to her husky voice extol the virtues of the collectibles and handicrafts to be found in Sutter Creek. After all, the general public had already been conditioned to paying for research and packaging costs. Once the word got out, somebody would make a bundle. He slid down further in the chair, cradling the receiver in the hollow of his shoulder.

"Matt? Are you there?"

"Yeah."

"Why are you so quiet? You don't like the idea?"

"I didn't say that."

"Of course you didn't. You haven't said *anything*."

"Where's Sutter Creek?" he asked obediently. He didn't care. If she wanted to go, they'd go.

"Where?" She sounded outraged. "Matt, this is your neck of the woods. How can you not know? It's famous. It's . . . *historical*."

His smile broadened to a grin. She was as passionate about geography and history as she was about everything else. "I think I've been there before," he soothed. "The name's familiar, but offhand I can't place it. Refresh my memory."

"It's in gold country." Now she sounded thrilled. "Matt, it's a perfect time to drive there. The hills should be covered with wildflowers." She hesitated briefly, then sped on. "Unless...you're not allergic to pollens, are you? If you are, it might cause a problem. But I hear they have some pretty good over-the-counter stuff now. Of course, if we were near the herb farm, Uncle Theo could whip up something for you."

"No allergies," he said firmly. "Where in gold country? It covers a lot of territory."

"South of Sacramento on Highway 49. Let me check the mileage." She paused, muttering at the map. "Um, I don't know," she said slowly, obviously having second thoughts. "Maybe it's too far. It would probably take us three hours to get there at least. Maybe more."

"We'll leave early."

"We'd have to leave at the crack of dawn," she objected. "You know how awful the traffic is in the morning. It takes hours just to get in or out of the city."

Matt ignored the exaggeration. "Then we'll leave at the crack of dawn. We could spend the night. That way it won't matter how long the drive is."

Matt waited. A long time. In the stark silence that followed, he experienced an overwhelming urge to see the expression on Kim's face. He would also have given a lot to know just what erotic images her fertile imagination was conjuring up.

"Don't even think about it, Kingsley," she said finally.

"What?"

"Innocence isn't your strong suit," she informed him.

He wondered just how often Kim Cassidy had to eat her words. "All I said was—"

"I heard you. Stay overnight, right?"

"Right. People who take business trips do it all the time. At least my people do." He waited. When she didn't say anything he added, "This *is* a business trip, right?"

The single-word reply was grudging. "Right."

"Then what's the problem? We go and look around. Spend a full day, hit some of the nearby towns then come back the following morning."

The silence on her end of the line made him think of a dog, hackles raised, checking out a new and possibly hostile territory.

"Two rooms." The words just begged him to argue.

"Of course," he said smoothly. "What else?"

Another silence. "What time?"

"Five-thirty. In the morning."

She sighed. "In the morning." A small click announced that she was gone.

Matt held the receiver, oddly reluctant to break the connection. When the silence became too much of a contrast to Kim's driving enthusiasm, he slowly dropped it in place.

It wasn't coming easily, but it was coming. She was beginning to trust him. A little. Reluctantly. Otherwise she wouldn't have agreed to spend the night away from her cozy little fortress.

Matt swung his chair around and gazed absently at the picture behind his desk. There wasn't a man in her life, at least not right now. He knew that for a fact. What convinced him was more than the knowledge that her time was entirely her own—it was the fact that Kim was too uneasy with the tension that sizzled between them. He knew from her startled glances and instinctive retreat that it had been a long time since she had dealt with such a sensual reaction. If ever.

That was fine with him, he mused, still surprised by the primitive surge of possessiveness that pumped through his veins at just the thought of her with another man. What surprised him even more was the fact that it was Kim, with her laughing eyes and take-charge attitude that brought it out in him. She wasn't his type. At least that would have been his opinion two weeks ago.

But then what did he know about types? *Nada.* There had been other women, none of them important. One in the past year, Susan. A woman who had needed to fill the emptiness in her life as much as he had. She had ended the comfortable and undemanding relationship six months earlier, and since then he had drifted into longer and longer workdays.

He had been reasonably content. He had learned one thing from Susan: Going alone to the social functions required by his job was better than linking up with a woman for the sole purpose of filling empty hours. It wasn't so much that he had been content, he realized now as he stared thoughtfully at the tree-lined hills of the picture. He had merely been existing. Attending to business, making all the right moves, doing everything that he had needed to do. And pulling out his blueprints and spending more and more time, as Mary so succinctly put it, in Shangri-la.

Then Kim had breezed into his office and turned his mundane, black-and-white life into glowing, shimmering color. Her business proposal, which initially seemed the height of absurdity, had caught him when he was feeling a bit jaded. Her love affair with the city of San Francisco, he found endearing. Her zest, her determination to make her mark in the city, fascinated him. He vaguely remembered that he had once felt the same way. When he had sampled her cooking, he'd known that she had the talent to make it big. And once he'd realized that she had the intelligence and business savvy to match it, he'd decided to help her pull off her dream.

But if he was anything, Matt was honest with himself. He rarely did things for altruistic reasons.

He wanted a successful restaurant, and she had exactly what it took to give him one. He also wanted Kim with a hunger and a need that astonished him.

And she wanted him.

She wasn't willing to admit it yet—not to herself or anyone else—but there it was. If she hadn't been interested, he would have chalked up his reaction at their first meeting to a case of overactive hormones and continued the interviews with his usual detached thoroughness.

But she was.

She was also incapable of concealing her feelings. She hadn't been able to hide the dazed pleasure in her eyes after they had kissed. She couldn't erase the sighs she'd breathed against his mouth, the feel of her hands moving through his hair, the soft strokes as she memorized the angles of his face with her fingertips.

That first kiss had been a turning point. For Matt, it merely confirmed what he'd already suspected: red-haired, green-eyed Kim was a small package of dynamite about to go off—and he wanted to be there when the explosion took place.

Unfortunately Kim's reaction hadn't been the same. Her wary expression said it all. She couldn't have made it clearer if she had spelled it out in words of one syllable: She didn't want a man messing up her life. Hands off. Business as usual. She had things to do and she wanted to be unencumbered while she did them.

Which made things difficult, but not impossible, Matt reflected. He had learned a long time ago that he was at his best in a tight spot.

His first priority after that kiss had been to bring back her jaunty confidence with him. He'd missed her artless commentaries on life. He wanted to hear whatever was running through her mind, not an edited version of what she thought was proper or prudent. Next he wanted her to trust him.

After that he wanted her clinging to him, her naked body under his.

And she knew it.

Kim slowly dropped the receiver in place, a frown drawing her brows together. He was doing it again. Pushing and prodding, nipping at her heels like a sheepdog until she was heading in the direction he wanted her to go. He was very good at what he did—pushing and prodding. He had an impressive string of successes in the business world to prove it. Not to mention the fact that she usually ended up doing precisely what he wanted her to do anyway.

She wasn't a fool. She knew what he was doing. The problem was, there was a definite time lag between his doing and her knowing. Matt was a lot more experienced at this kind of warfare than she was. And he had a characteristic that she was sadly lacking.

Subtlety.

She had about as much of that quality as a clove of garlic, while Matt maneuvered with all the delicacy of a whiff of lemon balm. She wondered idly if he played chess. He probably did. It involved the torturous kind of strategy that would appeal to him. Her first, and last, game had been a disaster. Her idea of entertainment was not maintaining hours of nerve-racking silence while keeping three jumps ahead of her opponent.

Kim folded the map and put it on the small table by the door. Sutter Creek had seemed like a good idea at the time, now she wasn't so sure. It was one thing to go out with him, knowing that at the end of the day she would be in her apartment and Matt in his, with locked doors and several miles between them.

It was another thing entirely to pack a bag and ride off with him, planning to spend the night. It didn't matter that they would be in separate rooms; there was an act of intimacy in the arrangement, an acceptance that was disturbing. And he knew it. She had the distinct impression that it was just another step in his game plan. One by one Matt was slowly, diligently knocking down the barriers she kept putting up.

He knew exactly what he was doing, she thought crossly. And she knew he knew. And what was even worse, he *knew* that she knew he knew.

Shaking her head, Kim stalked back to the computer. Scowling at the screen, she wondered how he expected her to handle all the business with the restaurant—which still didn't have a name—when he seemed to be spending all of his time thinking of ways to distract her. How could she concentrate on requisitions for kitchen supplies when he was gearing up for a grand seduction scene?

Poking a key to scroll back to the beginning, Kim moodily eyed the words on the screen while her mind mulled over the other problem. Seduction? He hadn't said the word aloud. But then it hadn't been necessary. It was gleaming in his gray eyes, written all over the strong planes of his face, in the tension of his hard body. He didn't even try to conceal it.

So what was the problem? She was twenty-seven and should be able to handle the situation with some degree of sophistication. She was free to live as she pleased, and Matt was a man of discrimination. She wouldn't have to worry about being safe with him.

That wasn't the problem. The problem was, plain and simple, that she *couldn't* handle it. Forget sophistication, forget savoir faire, don't even bother mentioning finesse. She couldn't do it.

It was obvious that Matt was able to channel his energy into different areas, putting out brush fires when and where they occurred, but she was different. She didn't like distractions. She had learned that fact very early in life. The way she worked most effectively was to concentrate on one project at a time and stick with it until it was finished.

There was another basic difference between them: she couldn't separate her emotions from her work. She gathered everything she had—enthusiasm, energy, emotion—and aimed it at her goal. It was definitely a package deal.

And right now her priority had to be the restaurant. Not an affair with Matt, however tempting that might be. She had promised him a top-notch restaurant, one that he would be proud of, and that was exactly what she intended to give him. She thought briefly of her aunts and their bedrock convictions about certain things. A promise made was a promise kept. Because of them, she didn't lightly give her word. When she did, she kept it. It was that simple.

Kim moved the cursor down the requisition form and changed ten wire whisks to an even dozen. Come hell or high water, she was going to give Matthew Kingsley his restaurant—preferably one with a name. And if she had to put her love life on hold to do it, so be it.

It would take a rare man to accept a situation like that. If there was such a man around, she doubted if his name was Matthew Kingsley. No, she knew it for a fact—he definitely wouldn't like the idea.

She stared blankly at the screen, seeing narrowed gray eyes instead of little green letters. Well, to be perfectly honest, she wasn't crazy about the idea either, but that was the way it had to be. He was too distracting, drained too much of her energy. She'd never get the job done if she allowed herself to become involved with Matt.

And she had promised.

The hum of the powerful motor had a hypnotizing effect. To combat it Kim turned to the next page in her organizer. She spared a quick glance for the blur of passing scenery. The rugged terrain was beautiful, clothed in the soft hues of spring. Even in a year characterized by drought, the trees and hillsides were dressed in bright green.

"What do you think of The Crown Jewel?" she asked.

"A little pretentious, don't you think?"

"Yeah, as a matter of fact I do. How about Kim's Kitchen?"

He slanted a disbelieving look at her. "You're not serious."

She sighed. "No. I'm just warming up. The Cable Car?" she asked tentatively.

"Hmm."

"What we need here," she said determinedly, "is some brainstorming. A little participation on your part wouldn't hurt. What are some of the things that people expect to experience when they come to San Francisco?"

"Earthquakes?" he asked helpfully, then grinned at her look of exasperation.

"Sure. We name something located at the top of a high rise *Earthquake?* We'd be lucky to give away dinners. Get serious."

Matt reached over and calmly confiscated the book. Before she could do more than glare, he tossed it in the back seat.

"Matt! I'm trying to work."

"I know. That's why I took it." He nodded at the road ahead. "Take a good look out there. You've had your nose in that book for the past two hours, and you're missing some of the most beautiful country in California. It's time for a break."

"I noticed it," she said, shooting him a lethal look. "It's very pretty."

"Pretty." He shook his head in disgust and took her hand, which promptly curled into a fist. Resting it on his jean-clad thigh, he straightened her fingers and held them down with his hand. "Relax, Kim. We've already done a full morning's work. Forget the book for a while."

She tugged at her hand and he tightened his grip. "You're going to suffer from burnout before the damn thing opens if you keep on like this. You're already ahead of the schedule you gave me, and I have a feeling that you've worked seven days a week to do it. Consider this trip time off for good behavior."

"I don't take time off when I'm in the midst of a project," she began.

"You do now," he told her calmly. "I want you in top shape when the restaurant opens."

Kim snatched her hand back and stared up at him with narrowed eyes. "Just tell me one thing. Would you have acted this way with Henri?"

Watching the road ahead, he said honestly, "The situation would never have come up. Henri knows how to relax, and he does it every chance he gets." His fingers tightened fractionally around the steering wheel, and he eased the car around a hairpin turn. "Any more questions?"

"Yeah. When are you going to stop for breakfast?"

Twenty minutes later Matt pulled up and stopped in front of a small rustic coffee shop called Mom's. "How does this look?"

Kim opened her door. "Like they might have a decent cup of coffee." When Matt held the screen door for her she murmured, "What do you think of the name? Short, cute and catchy. They'd probably never know if we borrowed it."

Mom's had more than good coffee. The waitress brought out a basket of miniature muffins to hold them over while they scanned the menus.

Kim eyed the basket with interest. She reached for a muffin and absently broke it in two. "These are cute. Whose expense account is this trip going on?"

"Why?"

"If it's yours, I'm going to shoot the works. If it's mine, I won't." She grinned and popped half the muffin into her mouth.

"I'll catch this one, you take the next."

"Good. I think I'll have... My God." Her voice was reverent.

"What?" Matt looked up.

"Taste this." She held out the other half of her muffin. "It's lemon poppy seed. It's also wonderful." She looked down at the basket. "Good grief, they're all different. It's a good thing they're small, we've got to try them all. Look at this," she gloated. "Blueberry."

Kim put aside her menu and broke each of the muffins in half. "This one," she sniffed delicately before passing Matt his portion, "has vanilla bean in it. Oh, look at the chunks of apple in this one."

She closed her eyes and chewed thoughtfully. "Matt," she said as the waitress stopped at their table, "if this cook does everything as well as she—"

"He," the waitress said helpfully.

"—he does muffins, we've found ourselves a rare treasure. Maybe we can forget about going on to Sutter Creek and just stay here." She opened her eyes and looked up at the waitress, peering at her name tag. "Are there any antique shops in town, Fran?"

"No." The waitress grinned. "But Sutter Creek isn't that far away. You can buzz back and forth for meals. You might even talk Pop into making a box lunch for you."

"Pop?" Kim's eyes sparkled with interest. "I've got to talk to this man. I'll take the baked eggs with tarragon, whatever fresh fruit you have and rye toast." She turned to Matt. "Be back in a minute."

She arrived with the food. Sliding back into her seat, she said, "It really is a Pop. He and his wife once ran this place together. After forty years Mom got tired of cooking. She said she had cooked for her parents, her kids, her husband and a million strangers, and she wanted to quit and go on a cruise."

She took a small bite of the eggs and closed her eyes in silent appreciation. "That man really knows his stuff." When she opened them she saw that Matt was equally absorbed in his omelet. "So Pop took her on a cruise and let other people feed her. When they came back Mom started putting an addition on their small house and he cut the business back to breakfasts and lunches so he could keep it going by himself. Now they're both happy." She ended her breathless account with a triumphant, "And we're going to exchange recipes."

Energy, Matt mused, not for the first time, taking another bite of his excellent omelet. It radiated from her in waves, charging the air around them. Pop could probably run his microwaves on what she was putting out. Even the waitress wanted to be closer to the source. She was edging nearer with the coffeepot, although she had just refilled their cups.

Kim lighted up the whole place and she wasn't even aware of it. Nor did she have the slightest idea that one look from her made his body hard and tight and damned uncomfortable in already snug jeans. He shifted and tried to concentrate on his omelet.

"What do you think?"

Kim was eyeing him expectantly, waiting for his verdict. He knew that she was talking about Pop, the food. Knew what she wanted to hear. He was working on a nice, innocuous response when she smiled. The smile did it.

"I think," he said carefully, "that I want to make love to you. I want your hands on me like they were the other night, only this time I want them *all* over me. I want you wrapped around me without a scrap of clothes between us." He paused, then added deliberately, "And just to set the record straight, I wouldn't have said that to Henri."

"I knew it!" Kim glared at him. "I *knew* it. If you think—"

A stream of coffee drizzled into Matt's cup. Matt and Kim looked up. The waitress, her hand steady as a rock, turned and deftly filled Kim's cup. Her voice was casual.

"How long you known him, honey?"

Kim blinked. "Two weeks."

"Don't do it."

"Do what?" she asked, her fury fading and her eyes narrowing in amusement. She wished she had a picture of Matt's face.

Fran plunked the coffeepot on the table. "Go to bed with him."

Looking at Matt thoughtfully, Kim said, "No?"

"No. Two weeks isn't long enough to get a handle on a guy." The waitress pulled up a chair and joined them at the table. "They may look okay—" she slanted a noncommittal look at Matt "—but as soon as they get what they want, off they go."

Kim nodded gravely. "You've got a point."

"I know I do." She patted Kim's hand.

"May I say something?" Matt asked politely.

Both women spoke at once. "No."

Fran took another look at Matt and reluctantly got to her feet. "You take your time, honey," she cautioned. "Don't let him rush you. Don't give in the first time he asks."

"It *isn't* the first time," Matt pointed out.

Kim smiled. "Thanks, Fran. I'll think about it."

"You do that, honey," she said, picking up the coffeepot. "Give it some long, hard thought, because I have a feeling he isn't going to give up."

"You're damned right he isn't," Matt murmured.

Six

"You know what I think?" Kim asked.

They had left their bags at the small Victorian bed and breakfast off the main road and were walking along the wood-planked sidewalk in Sutter Creek, heading for the antique stores.

Matt looked down at her laughing face. "You're really enjoying this, aren't you?"

"What, shopping? Or that little scene in Mom's?" Her eyes widened, amusement lurking in their green depths.

"You know damned well what I mean."

"I've forgotten it already."

"Sure you have." Resigned he asked, "All right, what do you think?"

She tugged at his hand. "Wait a minute. I want to go in here." She was already pushing open the door when Matt stopped her. He clamped his hand around her wrist and led her away from the glass front, stopping near a rustic bench. Kim leaned back against the wood-framed wall and looked up at him, blinking thoughtfully at his determined expression. She had been tweaking the tiger's tail for over an hour, and apparently he'd decided he'd had enough.

"What do you think?" he repeated, resting his palms on the wall beside her head, caging her in the circle of his arms.

Kim's eyes widened. He was too big. Standing this close to him, she felt very small and very feminine. And very hot and very crowded. Flustered, she tried to peer around his broad shoulders to see how much attention they were attracting. "I didn't mean we had to stop traffic to talk about it," she pointed out. "Come on, I want to go in the store." She pushed away from the wall and was stopped an inch later, her breasts against his chest.

Matt didn't move, but his gray eyes narrowed in pleasure at the contact. "Tough. You started it, now finish it. What do you think?"

"Okay, if you insist." Kim retreated, digging her back into the wall again, trying not to grin. He didn't want to talk about it and he didn't want to *not* talk about it. Teasing him might involve a few unexpected risks, she reflected, but it certainly was entertaining.

"I think your timing is lousy," she said cheerfully. "If you're plotting a red-hot seduction, it seems to me that you shouldn't announce it in front of a roomful of people."

"Not full," he murmured, bending his head and nuzzling her fragrant hair. "One old man nursing a cup of coffee at a corner table hardly constitutes a crowd."

"And the waitress," she reminded him breathlessly, turning her head when his breath warmed her cheek.

"Yeah," he admitted. "She was a problem."

Kim prodded at his chest with a slim finger. "Matt, I really don't think this is the place to carry on a conversation like this. Why don't we check out the store?"

"You've already told me my timing is rotten." When a tourist walked by, muttering an apology as he brushed against them, Matt moved nearer, crowding Kim closer to the wall. "So I might as well finish what I started."

"Matt—"

"I meant every word I said this morning." His voice roughened. "I want to love you. I want to pleasure you until you go crazy, until you beg for more, beg for me."

"Matt!" Her cheeks flushed and she looked around uneasily. "For heaven's sake, there are people—"

"But I won't until you're ready. Remember that. You're as safe with me as you want to be." He slid his palms to her cheeks and nudged her chin up until she met his eyes. "When the time is right, you'll know it and so will I." He dipped his head and brushed his lips over hers. "So until then, relax." He stepped back and gestured toward the store. "After you, lady."

Kim rushed through the door, catching sight of their reflections in an old, gilt-framed mirror. The sight of his lazy, satisfied grin did nothing to soothe her ruffled feathers. Yes, she decided, moving to the back of the store and scanning the furniture, there was a definite risk involved when one chose to tease a tiger.

The afternoon passed in a flurry of visits to the other stores in town. When they left the last one, Matt suggested that they backtrack to Amador City. It took only a few minutes to travel along the two miles of oak-dotted hillsides and descend into the small town.

"Any normal red-blooded American male would have called it quits hours ago," Kim grumbled a couple of hours later as they climbed back into Matt's 4x4. She secured her seat belt while he tucked his latest acquisition into the inevitable box on the back seat.

"Didn't anyone ever take you shopping when you were a kid?" she demanded. "Are you trying to make up for a lifetime of deprivation in one afternoon?" She pointed at a shop across the street and said in a martyred tone, "We missed that one. Sure you don't want to run over for a few minutes?"

Matt grinned and started the car. "It's closing," he told her. "They're all closing."

"Thank God." She gave a pitiful sigh. "If you have any compassion at all, any consideration for my broken body, you won't mention the word 'antique' again today. All I want to think about is my room, a long hot bath and dinner."

Three hours later, bathed, fed and rested, Kim sat next to Matt on a sofa in the library of the charming Victorian house that was their home for the night. They were the only guests, and their hostess had left them alone after showing them the book-lined room and asking them to turn out the lights when they retired.

"I give up," Kim declared, looking around the beautifully appointed room. "It's impossible to avoid the subject of antiques when you're literally surrounded by them."

"Good. Then maybe we can look at this." He leaned over and plucked a large glossy book from the coffee table.

"Let me guess." Kim sounded resigned. "Antiques?"

He nodded. "Nineteenth century. I just might learn something." He cupped his hand around her shoulder and urged her closer. "Move over here so you can see."

Kim slid over, accepting half the weight of the book on her thighs and propping her feet on the coffee table next to his. She wasn't really surprised, she decided after a moment's reflection. Matt was the type who would thoroughly research and investigate any subject he became interested in—even one that some people simply delved into for fun.

Matt felt warm and solid at her side. And more tempting than he could possibly know. His blue short-sleeved shirt and dark slacks were casual and elegant and had probably cost a fortune. The crisp dark hair on his arm brushed against her each time he turned a page, creating a starburst of sensation that shimmered through her veins with every movement.

"Can you imagine anyone using something as hideous as that!" Wide-eyed, Kim pointed to an elegant, curli-cued, molded Belleek tea set.

Matt looked down at her, eyeing her astonished expression thoughtfully. "I suppose it falls in the category of beauty being in the eye of the beholder. Why do I get the impression that you don't know any more about these things than I do?"

"Because I *don't* know any more about them than you do," she said promptly.

"I thought you were an expert."

"*I* never said that."

He closed the book with a snap and put it back on the table. Scowling he said, "You mean you've been dragging me—"

"Who's been dragging whom?"

"—through one store after another and you don't even know what we're looking for?"

Kim sighed in exasperation. "I know the *look* of what we're looking for. You said you wanted the restaurant to be just like my apartment, which is an exact replica of my home in Posy Creek. Ergo..." She paused, looking pleased

with herself. "One of my professors loved to say 'ergo,'"
she explained, laughing up at him, "and I hardly ever
manage to sneak it into a conversation. So, ergo, we're
looking for Posy Creek. Well, I just *do* happen to be an
expert on Posy Creek."

She snatched a breath and sped on. "I lived there all my
life, and my house is chock-full of stuff my parents and
their parents and *their* parents had. So I may not know the
names of all these doodads—" she waved at the book
"—but I know the real stuff when I see it. At least the
things that people have in Posy Creek."

She slanted another look up at him. "And it's pretty
obvious that we haven't found any, aside from your
knickknacks, I mean. Matt, maybe we should call in your
fancy decorator and have him start checking around."

There was a stubborn set to Matt's chin. "We're going
to do it ourselves."

"We're going to run out of time!"

"No we won't."

The furniture wasn't the object of all this running
around, he reminded himself. Somehow they would col-
lect what they needed. Kim was the reason he was holed up
in his office all hours of the day, driving Mary and the rest
of his staff crazy with midnight calls. He needed more time
with Kim. Alone.

He stared thoughtfully at the tips of his gleaming shoes,
considering his words. That was just part of the picture.
Kim needed time. With him. Whether she knew it or not.
Hell, even if she did know it she probably wouldn't admit
it, he reflected with a slight smile. She was almost as stubborn as he was.

She wanted him. He had seen her beautiful eyes gleam
with curiosity and heat and excitement when she looked at
him. He had also seen her tamp down the feelings with a

control that was extraordinary for a person who ran on impulse and instinct. Yeah, he told himself dryly, she wanted him all right, but she wasn't going to do one damn thing about it. Because of the restaurant.

The restaurant.

That could have been a miscalculation on his part, he decided with a belated flash of insight. Instead of removing the barriers between them, it had made them higher than ever.

Kim got to her feet, trying to hold back a yawn. "I'm beat. I'm going to bed."

Matt followed her to the door and turned off the lights. "Speaking of bed . . ."

"No." Even in the dim light on the stairway he could see the amusement behind the determination.

"No?"

"No." She moved up the stairs ahead of him.

He kept his voice light. "All I wanted was—"

"No."

"—to tell you that I have a water bed. If you don't and want to trade, I'll be noble."

"No way, Kingsley." Her grin when she looked down at him was smug.

"What do you mean?"

"I mean whatever the landlady told you about my bed, forget it. I'm not going to trade."

Intrigued, Matt took the stairs two at a time and caught up with her. "She didn't tell me anything."

"Hah! Then why are you trying to talk me into switching?" Kim stopped at her door, her hand on the knob, eyeing him suspiciously.

She had a right to be skeptical, Matt reflected, watching her lean back against the door, a smile teasing the corners of her mouth. As usual her instincts were good; they just hadn't taken her far enough. He didn't give a damn about switching rooms or beds with her.

He wanted to share one.

If he couldn't do that, he'd settle for whatever was being offered. For now. And if that meant watching her laugh while she talked about bedrooms and beds, so be it. It was another small step.

His brows rose and he moved a step nearer. "You going to show me what you have in there?"

She grinned. "You can't talk me out of it. Understand?"

He raised his right hand. "I won't even try."

"Okay." After one last doubtful glance Kim unlocked the door and threw it open. She led him into the room and pointed. Four sturdy chains hung from the beams and were secured to the corners of the bed.

"Well, I'll be damned." Matt's startled comment pleased her.

She gave the bed a nudge, a look of immense satisfaction crossing her face when it swung gently back and forth. "Ta-dah!" she crowed. "It's like a hammock."

Matt looked from her to the bed and back again. "What a waste," he muttered. "Have you thought—"

"Matt." It was a warning. She glanced at him in disgust. Of course she had thought. Did he think she was *dense?* That was the reason she hadn't gotten the rest she'd needed earlier: she *had* been thinking. Of his big body sprawled on the bed beside her. Of the heat and promise in his gray eyes.

Kim gave herself a shake. "Bedtime," she said briskly.

"Yeah." Matt took one last look at the swaying bed and walked over to the open door. He waited for her. When she came closer, he settled back against the jamb. "Are you going to kiss me good-night?"

Kim walked into his open arms. Yes. She was definitely going to kiss him good-night.

Close as she was he drew her closer, into the cradle of his parted legs, until she was off balance and clinging to him, resting against the undeniable evidence of his arousal. His large hand cupped her nape, then tangled in the fragrant mass of her hair.

At the touch of his fingers Kim stilled, a heady sense of awareness sizzling through her. "I can't go to bed with you," she murmured, lifting her face to his.

"Won't," he corrected, running his thumb along her lower lip.

"Won't." It was a sigh of agreement, barely a sound at all.

He slid his hand down the silky fall of her hair and wrapped a long strand around his finger, his gaze frankly possessive. "Someday," he promised.

"Mmm?" She was leaning against him, his long arm holding her in place against his hard frame, his hand cupping her bottom. Kim tucked her cheek in the hollow of his shoulder, listening to his heartbeat. Her eyes slitted in hazy satisfaction. It was pounding as fast as hers was.

"Soon." He ran a thumb down the length of her elegant spine, smiling when she shuddered.

"Matt?"

"Mmm?"

"We'd be crazy to—"

"Kiss me, Kim." He didn't want to hear whatever logical, rational objection she was going to offer. He wanted her swarming all over him, dazzling him with her warmth and laughter, focusing all of her reckless energy on him. On him alone. Binding him in a tangle of honeyed, fragrant limbs. "Kiss me."

Her lips brushed his, lingering.

His arm tightened. "Again."

"Damn it, Matt." She sounded desperate. "How do you do this to me? I don't want it." Kim wrapped her arms around his neck, stretching along his lean length, dizzy from his heat and reeling from the touch of hands that traced her curves in a tantalizing line from her breasts down to her thighs. Slowly, almost reluctantly, she brushed her mouth against his again, tasting warmth, wine and desire. His arms tightened, one hand cupping her head, holding her close.

A long time later he lifted his head, his eyes gleaming with masculine satisfaction. "You don't want this? The hell you don't, lady," he muttered. "The hell you don't."

A week later Kim poked her head through the outer office door. She wore hunter-green slacks and a long-sleeved silky blouse in a paler shade. A handful of gold chains shimmered at her neck. "Hi, Mary."

Matt's secretary looked up from her computer, a harried expression on her face. "Hi."

"Is he in?"

"Unfortunately."

"Uh-oh, one of those days?"

Mary rolled her eyes. "One of those *weeks.*"

Kim stepped in and closed the door behind her. "I guess it's a good thing I've kept my distance lately, huh?"

"At least it shows you have a keen sense of self-preservation." The intercom buzzed at her elbow. "You know," Mary said conversationally, "we ordered that thing because it had a nice, muted buzz. As far as I know, Matt's the only one who can make it sound like a nest of hornets." She pressed a button. "Yes, Matt."

"Do you have the latest figures from Kim?"

Kim winced at the sound of his hard voice and hastily dropped her weekly report in front of Mary.

"It's on my desk," Mary said calmly, grinning at the younger woman.

"When did she leave it?" he snapped.

"Just a while ago."

"Damn it!"

"There's no need to swear, Matt. I was going to bring it right in."

An exasperated sigh came through the intercom and both women grinned. "Sorry, Mary. I wanted to see Kim."

The secretary waved Kim to a chair. "I doubt if she's gone far. Want me to track her down?"

"Please."

"Oh, Matt?"

"Yeah?"

"Do you need her to bring anything? Anything other than her report, I mean."

"No." He paused. "Just tell her to get her sweet little tail in here."

"Okay." Mary tapped a button on the machine and leaned back, raising her brows at Kim. "You heard?" When Kim nodded she narrowed her eyes. "You wouldn't be the cause of all the snarling in there, would you?" She gestured in the general direction of Matt's door.

"Me?" Kim looked startled. She tapped a fingernail thoughtfully on the arm of the chair, then shook her head. "Nope. I couldn't be. I haven't even seen him for a week. It's probably just his normal sweet disposition coming through." The two women exchanged droll looks.

Mary ran a hand through her silver hair. "I swear, there are days when he outdoes his father."

Kim settled deeper into the chair, rapt interest on her face. "Who was a benevolent and kindly man, right?"

"Wrong. On the best of days he was a barracuda. If someone crossed him, he really got nasty."

"My, my. A lovely legacy to pass on. Is Papa, along with his irascible genes, still around?"

Mary nodded. "Mellowed considerably since he retired. Now, when he isn't golfing or puttering with his begonias, he follows his wife around telling her how to do all the things she'd been doing beautifully for years."

Kim leaned forward. "And Mama? What does she do?"

"Tells him to stick his advice in his ear." Mary smiled. "Actually they're quite devoted to each other." The gray box on her desk snarled again and Mary slanted an exasperated look at Kim. Reaching out and poking a button, she said, "Yes, Matt?"

"Haven't you found Kim yet?"

"She just walked in."

"Well, tell her to—"

"Yes, Matt." She cut him off and leaned over to pick up the folder Kim had dropped on her desk. "You might as well take this in with you."

Kim took the report and moved to the inner door. She stopped with her hand on the knob and turned back to Mary. "Any suggestions?"

Mary smiled. "About what?"

"How to deal with a testy tiger?"

"That's the way you think of him?" Mary's smile broadened.

"Testy?"

"No. A tiger."

Kim nodded.

"Interesting."

The box buzzed again and Kim scowled. "Come on, Mary, give."

"Try injured innocence."

"That's it?" Kim looked doubtful. "That's all?" The box vibrated impatiently. Giving it a lethal look, she said, "If that were my desk, I'd rip that sucker out by the entrails." Mary's surprised laughter followed her through the door.

"Hi, Matt." Kim dropped the file on the corner of his desk and took a seat across from him.

Matt was writing on a large yellow pad in angry slashes. He looked up, his eyes slitted dangerously. "Where the hell have you been?"

Injured innocence, Kim reminded herself. She crossed her legs and smoothed the crease of her slacks. "Home. Working."

Matt did not look impressed.

"That is, when I wasn't running around dickering with the various vendors you introduced me to last week," she continued. "It's all in there." She nodded at the folder on his desk.

Matt scowled. "You haven't answered your phone."

"I couldn't if I wasn't home," she pointed out in a reasonable tone. "But I left the answering machine on," she added virtuously.

Matt scrawled a final word on the pad, pressing so hard on the pencil that the led tip flew off and bounced against the wall. "A hell of a lot of good that does if you don't return the calls."

Kim blinked, watching the lead fall and embed itself in the ivory carpet. "I did," she protested. "It's not my fault that you weren't here. I left a message with Mary."

"Several, if my memory serves me right." He got up and stalked over to the window. "You couldn't take time off to look for furniture last Sunday. You couldn't have dinner with me Monday or Tuesday. And you couldn't go to a reception with me last night. I know it was a last-minute invitation, and I apologize for that, but I'd just remembered the invitation."

He didn't *sound* apologetic, Kim reflected. He still sounded mad enough to bite. "So you *did* get them. All of them." Her tone asked, "So what's the problem?"

He turned away from the window and gave her a level look. "Yes, I got them. I didn't like any of them. I thought we had a deal, had agreed on certain conditions. One of which was that we would be finding furniture for the restaurant."

She nodded. "We did. We do," she amended conscientiously. "I just had to make some priority decisions this week."

"Oh?" Matt came back and perched on the corner of his desk, crossing his arms on his chest.

Kim nodded eagerly. "All of those vendors were clamoring for appointments. They were also willing to cut each other's throats for a slice of the business, so I had to strike while they were hot."

"Who did you go with?" he asked, diverted.

"We had it narrowed down to five, but Robinson and Deluth offered the best deals."

He nodded. "Good choice." His voice hardened again. "What does that have to do with last Sunday?"

Kim took a deep breath, not bothering to hide her annoyance. "I spent the day touring their facilities."

His eyes narrowed. "And Monday and Tuesday nights?"

"I let them wine and dine me while we hammered out a contract."

"I suppose you were also wheeling and dealing during the reception last night?"

Kim lowered her lashes. The reception. That was a weak point, she admitted silently. She simply hadn't wanted to go. As far as that went, she *could* have scheduled the other things differently during the week. But she hadn't. She had simply needed some time away from Matt. Time to work undisturbed, and she had grasped at any excuse.

The cutthroat antics of Robinson, Deluth and friends had by contrast, been a welcome relief. She had gladly gone along with their suggested appointments. The reception at one of Matt's competitor's hotels, celebrating the opening of a new health spa, had been a horse of another color.

She had known it would be a glittering event, a gathering of San Francisco's elite—a small nucleus of people who were linked by business and social commitments. It was the type of event she was rarely invited to, usually only in the line of business—if it involved a restaurant and she knew one of the chefs. She avoided such occasions whenever possible. The people attending were undoubtedly nice—or so she told herself. She simply had nothing in common with them, no reason to mingle with them.

And Matt was an eligible male, born and raised in the center of that tight circle.

If she had shown up on Matt's arm wearing the elegant, quietly sexy dress she reserved for such occasions, there would have been more than a few elevated brows. The owners of the brows would have ranged from disgruntled mothers to those of either sex who would smile knowingly when she explained that she was the manager of Kingsley's new restaurant. It hadn't taken much thought; she had decided that she simply didn't need that kind of aggravation.

"No," she said slowly, "I wasn't wheeling and dealing. I was burning the midnight oil to finish this report. I was also trying to clear up a few things so I could go away for a couple of days. Maybe four or five."

Matt went still, then moved back to his chair. "Go where?"

Relieved that the question of the reception seemed to be behind them, Kim brightened. "Home. To Posy Creek."

"And when were you going to tell me?" he asked grimly.

"Today. That's why I hung around."

"Why?"

Kim frowned. "Why was I going to tell you? It was the only thing to do. I couldn't just disappear. After all—"

He interrupted ruthlessly. "Why are you going?"

"Oh. Aunt Valerian called yesterday morning. She wouldn't come right out and say it, but I think she and Aunt Primrose are lonely."

Valerian? Primrose? Matt's eyes narrowed again. "You're not serious."

Kim stared at him, puzzled. "Why wouldn't I be? I think they miss Uncle Theo. They're awfully close, you know." Her brows drew together in thought. "They keep busy during the day. Aunt Valerian is working on a new shampoo using rosemary oil, and Aunt Primrose has just finished a batch of lavender candles. They have a refreshing, antiseptic fragrance—the candles, not my aunts—and Aunt Primrose gives them to people to burn in sickrooms. I think it's the evenings when they miss Uncle Theo the most."

Matt nodded.

"And you know I *did* promise. I told Uncle Theo that I'd look in on them when I could."

He nodded again, some of the tension easing from his shoulders. "And you always keep your promises."

"I really do need to go." Kim's glance slid over his shoulder. "And there's something else I need to ask you."

Matt stiffened. "Why don't you try looking at me instead of the window while you ask?"

Her anxious gaze swung back to him. "How would you feel about giving me carte blanche with the furniture?"

"Why?"

Kim was startled by the bleak look on his face. "Well," she hesitated, "that's another thing that Aunt Valerian told me. Old Mrs. Beaumont died, a neighbor."

He touched her shoulder with a gentle hand. "I'm sorry. Were you close to her?"

"In Posy Creek we're—"

"I know," he sighed. "Close to everybody."

"But that's not the reason."

"Are you going back for the funeral?"

"Oh, no." She shook her head. "She was cremated last week. She—"

"Then what's the problem?"

"*Matt.*" Sheer exasperation sharpened her voice. "Will you please just let me finish? Although I was very fond of Mrs. Beaumont, she was ninety-eight. Uncle Theo and the aunts had kept her alive with herbs for the past ten years. At least that's what she claimed."

Kim thought about that for a second, then shrugged. "Whatever. Anyway, she had no family, and the only thing she really loved was her obnoxious, overweight, little yipping dachshund."

Matt settled back in his chair. Lacing his hands over his flat stomach, he waited.

"She told my aunts to have the dog put to sleep when she died because no one else would give it the TLC that she had."

"And they did?"

"Of course. And that brings us to the next point. She also directed the aunts to buy Tonto—"

"The dog?" Matt hazarded.

"Of *course*." Kim was beginning to look frayed around the edges. "—to buy Tonto a grave and a headstone in the local pet cemetery."

Matt blinked.

"And to leave an annuity of some sort for his perpetual care." She took a deep breath. "To fund the annuity, she told the aunts to have an estate sale. Everything she had was to go."

The amusement faded from Matt's eyes. "And?" he asked softly.

"And, since I had been at her beck and call for years, running her errands and hauling Tonto to the vet, I could go in before the sale and buy whatever I wanted."

"When do we leave?" he asked softly.

Seven

Kim stared at Matt. He hadn't moved from his chair. "What do you mean, 'when do we leave?' *I'm* leaving in the morning."

"I'll pick you up."

"Matt—"

"You're not going without me." His even voice told her he meant what he said.

"Why not?" Kim bristled, glaring at him across the width of the desk. She expected a reply that said in essence, "because I'm the boss." Instead his boyish smile disarmed her.

"Because I want to help you pick out the furniture."

Stunned, she said, "But you can't just pick up and leave on such short notice!" Then she blinked as a smile was mirrored in his gray eyes.

"I'm the boss," he reminded her. "I can do anything I damn well please."

"You have things to do." She waved a hand that took in his office and the hotel at large. "Meetings. Responsibilities." That smile, she decided grimly, should be registered as a lethal weapon.

"So do you."

Kim stiffened. "And I worked most of last night attending to them. You know I wouldn't take off if I had things hanging fire."

"Neither would I." He leaned forward and pressed a button on the intercom. "Mary, would you book me a room at the—" He looked at Kim. "What's the name of the hotel?"

Her eyes widened in surprise. "There's no hotel in Posy Creek."

"Motel?"

She shook her head.

Matt sighed. "Bed and breakfast?"

"Nope."

"Forget it, Mary," he said shortly. He got to his feet and walked to the end of the room, shoving his hands in his pants pockets and staring out of the window. Kim joined him, peering down with interest at the ant-sized people scrambling up and down the sidewalks and across the streets. People in the city were always in a hurry, she reflected, watching a cable car labor up the hill. They were probably too busy to even stop and watch a sunset or—

"What's your house like?"

Kim had lifted her gaze and was concentrating on a gull soaring on a thermal. She answered absently. "A big old place. It rambles on forever." She stopped and took a deep breath, closing her eyes in self-disgust. While she waited for what was inevitably to follow, she concluded that a master negotiator like Matt must find the present game a bit lackluster. She was no challenge at all.

"How would you like a houseguest?"

As usual there was no beating around the bush with Matt. Everything was straightforward, out in the open. How would she like a houseguest? About as much as she'd like a case of ptomaine.

Kim considered her options. As far as she could see they boiled down to yes and no. A yes would result in a whole bunch of trouble—a no in a lost argument, *then* a whole bunch of trouble.

She looked up and met his speculative gaze. "Sure." She gave him a challenging smile. "Why not?"

"How much farther?"

At Matt's lazy question, Kim tore her gaze from the tumble of oaks and manzanita along the side of the road. Behind them towered a thick stand of sentinel-straight eucalyptus. As the big 4x4 sped by them, the strobelike effect of sun and shadow on Matt's lean face provided a dramatic contrast to the soft greenery all around them. The air was warm, the sun still spring mild.

"Not far. We'll be there soon," she promised, closing her eyes and inhaling deeply. When she opened them, Matt was smiling.

"Smell like home?"

She nodded, anticipation brightening her eyes. "I'd know it anywhere. I could be blindfolded and told I was in another country, but all it would take is one whiff and I'd know exactly where I was."

Matt considered the sweeping statement, then sniffed appreciatively. "What is it?"

"A little bit of everything." She stared ahead at the dips and turns of the winding road. "Sun mixed with rain, dust and sandy soil. Trees. Fields of herbs." She shrugged. "It's Posy Creek."

"We could bottle it and make a fortune." Matt remembered that he had once thought the same thing about Kim.

"Get ready to slow down," Kim warned, tapping his arm for emphasis. "I want you to pull over in a minute." She pointed to a wide shoulder at the crest of the hill. "Now! Right there."

Matt nosed to a stop beneath an ancient live oak and killed the motor. "Now what?"

"Now," Kim said, opening her door and sliding to the ground, "you take your first look at Posy Creek."

Matt slammed his door and stepped over to Kim's side, watching her face rather than the scene spread out below them. Her barely concealed excitement, the utter familiarity of her movements told him that this was not something she was doing just for his benefit. He had the distinct feeling that whenever she returned home this was a ritual she performed. More than a ritual, he decided, taking another look at her pensive face. Almost a pilgrimage.

Then Matt glanced down at Posy Creek.

It looked like a child's miniature town, except the houses weren't uniform and boxlike, and they weren't sparkling with new paint. They rambled with wings and ells and wide, hospitable porches that had been added over the years. Most of them were white, with white picket fences and large shade trees dotting the yards.

A narrow asphalt road bordered by the purple haze of jacaranda trees meandered up and down and around the hills, eventually touching the long dirt driveway of each home. One end of the road headed north, where he assumed it eventually joined up with the town.

If the helter-skelter, almost whimsical, patterns of the split-rail fences were any indication, the property lines must play merry hell with the local tax assessor, he thought idly. Weathered houses sat in the midst of green fields, defying any suggestion of symmetry. There was no order, but there was harmony. There was a tranquility rarely thought of and impossible to find in the frenetic bustle of any city.

Matt surveyed the cluster of homes cupped by the surrounding hills with unblinking intensity. This was it, he thought, dazed. Call it by any name—Eden, Shangri-la, Camelot—this was it.

And he wanted it with the same gut-wrenching need that had clawed at him the first time Kim had walked through his office door.

"Nice, huh?"

Kim's voice jolted him. Nice? He looked down to see if she was serious. Her soft, pleased expression told him that she was. *Nice,* for God's sake.

"Yeah, it's nice."

She grabbed his hand and tugged him back toward the car. "Come on. I want you to meet the aunts."

As they descended into the hollow, Kim broke the silence in the car. "Matt?" Her voice was hesitant.

"Hmm?"

She looked across at him uncertainly. "I just wanted to warn—talk to you about my aunts."

"Oh?" He raised his brows. Warn?

"Well, it's just that they've lived in Posy Creek all of their lives."

He nodded. "Uh-huh."

"They do things . . . differently."

"I see." His fingers flexed on the steering wheel as they rounded a steep curve.

Kim frowned, a look of growing determination on her face. "No, I don't think you do."

"Okay," he said amiably. "Tell me what I don't see. Are we talking unique and distinctively different?"

Kim shot him a glum look. "We're talking peculiar."

Matt grinned and tried again. "Kim, I've lived in the city all of my life, right?"

She nodded.

"If they visited me, they'd probably think that I do some odd things. And since I'm a bit out of my element here, I'll probably—"

"No," she interrupted, "if you had lived next door to them all of your life, you'd still think that they were..."

"What?"

"Weird. Lovable," she assured him blithely, "but undeniably weird."

He was still chuckling when he followed her pointed finger and turned into a long driveway. The large white house at the end seemed almost as welcoming as the two elderly ladies who traipsed down the stairs with glad cries.

"Kim!"

They waited impatiently for the car to roll to a stop, then engulfed Kim in hugs the moment her feet hit the ground. Matt closed his door and leaned against a dusty black fender, watching, a smile on his face. Nothing weird here, he observed. It looked like a normal, affectionate homecoming. The same kind he received when he went home, at least from his mother; his father settled for a handshake and a hearty clap on the shoulder.

The aunts didn't look peculiar. They were whippet thin, deeply tanned and shared the same high cheekbones and pug noses. The combination gave them an ingenuous, if perpetually surprised, look. Although they both wore their hair tied back, one's was a lustrous gray, one's a strident orange. They each wore denim jumpers with a multitude of bulging pockets.

Kim returned the hugs with enthusiasm, and the three women all began talking at once. Kim slipped her arms around their waists and, with a last blink at the tangerine glory topping off one of the aunts, turned them toward Matt. "Aunt Valerian, Aunt Primrose, I'd like you to meet my boss, Matthew Kingsley. Matt, my aunts."

Two sets of bright blue eyes assessed him. Taking their time, they inspected him from his running shoes and jeans to his oxford shirt and the sunglasses he was tucking into his pocket.

"Boss?" The gray-haired aunt met his steady gaze and studied him. She sounded skeptical. Or hopeful. Matt wasn't sure which.

He nodded, pushing himself away from the car to shake first one capable hand then the other. "Among other things."

The sisters blinked. Their expressions were identical—anticipation, Matt decided. "What kind of other things?" they chorused.

Lover. Almost. Soon. "Friend."

The two women commiserated with a glance.

"We turn the girl loose in a city crawling with young, upwardly mobile young men and all she brings home is a friendly employer," muttered the one with the orange hair. "I ask you now, how are we ever going to have children running wild in Posy Creek if all she ever thinks about is work?"

"That's a problem," he agreed, shooting a glance at Kim's resigned face. "I'll work on it."

"Aunt Primrose," Kim suggested to carrot top, "you just might be embarrassing my guest."

Valerian resumed her intense survey of him. Matt grinned at her. She grinned back. "I don't think this one's easily embarrassed," she said to Kim. "If *you* think so, I'd say you don't know him very well. Not as well as you should if you're bringing him home to meet us."

"I'm not—"

Valerian lifted her chin. "Young man, just what are your intentions?"

Kim groaned.

Matt took in the hopeful expressions of the two old women. "The worst," he assured them.

"Heh, heh, heh," Primrose chortled. "There's hope yet!"

Valerian's sharp glance was thoughtful. Linking her arm through Matt's, she urged him toward the house. "Come in and have some tea. You can have your choice—damiana, ginseng, magnolia or orchid."

"Aunt Valerian!"

The old woman hustled Matt along. Looking over her shoulder, she soothed, "Just joking, child. Just joking."

"You'd better be." Falling behind them, Kim murmured, "What happened to your hair, Aunt Primrose?"

"An experiment, child. I wanted to see if henna really worked." She paused then added dryly, "It does."

The older women busied themselves filling glasses with ice and tea. When they brought them to the table, Kim took two glasses and sniffed the contents carefully before handing one to Matt.

Valerian grimaced. "Really, Kim!"

Kim grinned at her. "Just keeping you honest."

Matt watched the byplay with raised brows, shrugging when it became obvious that neither of the women were going to share the joke.

Primrose plopped a plateful of lumpy cookies in front of Matt and demanded, "Tell us about the new restaurant."

Kim's face lighted up. "It's everything I dreamed about when I left here. You'll have to come for the grand opening."

Matt leaned back, watching her animated face. "Stay at the hotel as my guests," he murmured. "In fact, come anytime. There'll always be a room for you."

The aunts looked at his contented smile, following his gaze to their glowing niece before they exchanged a deeply satisfied glance. "Thank you," they said together. "We will."

Kim slid Matt a teasing smile. "What with his money and my brilliance," she told her aunts, "we're going to make it a real showpiece. Matt wants it to look like my apartment, so—"

"But that looks just like your house," Primrose protested. "Why not go for something modern, something different that young city people will enjoy?"

Kim gave a small shrug. "Matt's convinced that they *will* like it, so we've been scouring all the local antique shops for old chests and hutches."

"A waste of time," Valerian declared. "And money. Especially with Mrs. Beaumont's house full of things to choose from."

"That's one of the reasons we're here," Kim admitted. "But the more I think about it, the more I wonder if..." Her voice dwindled away and she stared thoughtfully at her glass while the others watched her.

"If you don't feel right about it, then forget it." Matt's decisive words broke the small silence.

Kim looked up at him, a flicker of gratitude warming her eyes. She also seemed a bit surprised at his sensitivity, Matt reflected a bit grimly.

"I don't know how I feel," she admitted. "I just wish I knew what Mrs. Beaumont really expected—or wanted—me to do. I just don't know," she repeated slowly.

The aunts looked at each other. "Did you—" Valerian began.

Primrose shook her head. "Not yet."

Valerian got up, trotted over to a pine hutch and began scrabbling through a series of small drawers. "Now where did I put it?" she murmured, shoving one paper-filled drawer shut and opening another. "Ah!" She pulled out a crumpled envelope and turned, waving it triumphantly. "Here it is."

Handing it to Kim, she explained, "It's from Mrs. Beaumont. She gave it to us several months ago. For you."

Kim was turning the letter over when Primrose jumped to her feet. "Read it later," she suggested. "When you have time to think. Right now we want you to see something. Matt, bring your tea and come along. We're going to show you the gardens."

She led the way out the back door saying, "They're open to the public three days a week so it seems we're always out here keeping things tidy."

"They're also my aunts' pride and joy," Kim muttered as she trailed him out the door, sliding the letter into her canvas tote.

They were also big, a couple of acres, Matt estimated. And lovely. It was actually a series of small gardens joined by an intricate series of walkways. He was looking at far more than a hobby, he realized. It was concrete evidence of dedication, of a lifetime of work and care.

"Kim, you'll be interested in this," Primrose said. "We just planted it." She pointed to a large colorful circle bordered with bricks. "Ten varieties of thyme are in there," she explained to Matt as they crunched their way along the winding track. "Are you wondering why all our paths are gravel?"

He nodded obediently.

"Gravel attracts the warmth."

He thought about that. "That's good?" he finally asked.

She nodded. "Very. The warmth intensifies fragrances." She tugged at his arm. "No, it's all right, you don't have to step over that." She pointed to the green, soft-textured ground cover that Matt was trying to avoid. "It's chamomile, a creeping herb. We have it in the paths because it sends up a delightful aroma when people walk on it. Don't worry, you can't hurt it. And these—" she touched several leafy bushes as she strode by a star-shaped plot "—are bee balm. We planted them throughout the garden because they attract hummingbirds."

Valerian pointed to a square of tightly clipped herb hedges arranged in intricate patterns. "Most of our visitors like the knot garden. They were very popular during the Renaissance."

"Do we need anything at the store before we go home?" Matt turned the key in the ignition and deftly backed the big car out of the aunts' driveway.

Kim's brows rose. We? Home? He was sure settling in fast. "No, I called my neighbor Mrs. Thatcher and asked her to get some things for me. She waters my plants and generally keeps the place ready for me."

"Sounds expensive, having someone keep it ready for you to drop in at a moment's notice."

"Not really. Anyway, you pay me a pretty good salary. Especially now. I can afford it." Her shrug was a casual movement of her slim shoulders. "Besides, whether I'm here or not, it's my home and it deserves to be taken care of."

She pointed left when they came to the fork. "That way. The first driveway."

Matt pulled up in front of a white house and turned off the motor. It was exactly as she had said, large and rambling. But only someone who had spent his or her whole life in the lovely old place could describe it with those two careless words. Camphor and sycamore trees spread their branches to shade the two-story house, and wildflowers rather than grass covered the ground sloping down to the road.

He pulled the luggage out of the back and dumped it on the wide wraparound porch. When Kim unlocked the door, he stepped inside and gazed at the bright, plant-filled room. Sheer lace curtains let the sunlight stream in through the windows, while white miniblinds provided the necessary privacy. Gleaming plank floors, bright cushions and oriental rugs, white wicker chairs and polished old chests completed the picture.

Matt finished his survey with a deep sense of satisfaction. Yes, he thought again. This is it.

"I'll show you the rest later," Kim said briskly. "Right now we have a date with a sunset." Matt set the luggage inside the door and followed her.

"I like your aunts," he said a few minutes later. He was sitting in a sturdy wicker chair with his feet crossed on the porch rail.

"And so you should." Kim leaned back with a contented sigh watching the sun drop to the top of a distant hill. She sat in the chair beside him. "They plied you with tea, fed you their infamous persimmon cookies and told you all about my misspent youth. What more could a visiting boss need?"

"You in my lap while we watch the sunset?"

"Forget it." No, that was something that neither of them needed. He was already using words like "home" and "we," implying that they were a couple. And she wasn't blind. She had been watching him when he'd told Valerian he was a friend. The word had been innocent, the expression in his eyes hadn't.

She had had doubts about the arrangement from the beginning, she remembered, gazing thoughtfully at the dramatic slashes of red in the sky. She had been right. She could feel it in her bones. Matt was not going to spend the next few days acting like her good friend or a prototype of the boy next door. Excitement surged through her at the thought.

Promptly squashing it, she turned to him saying, "If you liked the aunts so much, why were you in such a hurry to leave? If you had played your cards right, they would have pulled out the elderberry wine."

"We'll go back for it," he promised. "I wanted to see your house while it was still light. Sit on your porch and watch the sunset."

"Oh." Kim relaxed, crossing her ankles on the rail beside Matt's. "So what do you think of the house? What you've seen so far, I mean."

Matt reached out and took her hand, lacing his fingers through hers until their palms met. "It reminds me of you."

Kim looked up in surprise. "Me?"

"It's open and warm. And sexy." It was also exactly what he'd expected.

She stared at him.

His fingers tightened around hers. "It's also full of feminine charm, and it opens its arms to welcome a man. It has a lot of love for the right person."

Kim cleared her throat. "We *are* talking about the house?"

"Among other things." He smiled blandly at her disconcerted expression. "Where did your Mrs. Beaumont live?" he asked, changing the subject abruptly.

Kim nodded in the direction of the setting sun. "Over behind those hills. Her place backs up to the base of the mountain. It's a fair drive from the rest of us, but she liked her privacy. All told, she has—had—about a hundred acres."

"What'll happen to it now?"

A frown drew Kim's brows together. "I suppose it's going to be sold along with everything else. That could be a problem," she admitted. "No one around here really needs any more land, but we don't want developers to get their grubby little hands on it, either."

"When's the sale?"

"Sometime next week, I suppose."

Matt gazed at the gold-rimmed sky with appreciation. "That gives you a few days to look the place over and decide what you want."

"Yeah." She nodded moodily. "I feel like a ghoul going in there and picking over her things."

"She must have wanted you to do it. Otherwise she would have made other provisions."

"I know," Kim said slowly. "She first mentioned it to me years ago, and after that she reminded me about every six months. Logically I know it's what she wanted. In fact I promised her that I'd help take care of things when the time came. I just . . . never thought I'd ever be doing it."

He moved her hand to his thigh, covering it with his. "Will it be hard for you, going through her place? Do you want me to come along?"

Kim nodded gratefully. "Thanks, I'd like that. Although it won't be hard in the sense that you mean. At least I don't think so. Mrs. Beaumont was a brisk, no-

nonsense lady who would rather argue than lapse into sentimentality. Our relationship was cordial, but I don't know if it ever got any warmer than that."

Matt smiled, rubbing a thumb absently over the back of her hand. "I can't imagine you being lukewarm about anyone."

Kim's expression was wry. "You're right. She was a formidable old woman, a hard nut to crack, but I never gave up trying. My feelings veered from one extreme to the other. I admired her for her grit and independence and I felt sorry for her because she was alone. I'd go out of my way to help her, and then get resentful because she didn't seem grateful. Uncle Theo always said that Mrs. Beaumont was put on this earth to build character in the rest of us."

"Sounds like a philosophical man," Matt said, gazing at the disappearing sun.

"That he is." Kim absently tugged on her hand. It felt fine right where it was, but there was no sense in giving him any ideas. "Of course, Mrs. Beaumont considered that a rare compliment. She said the world needed more character. And who knows, maybe she was right." She gave the horizon one last lingering look and got to her feet. "Come on, I'll show you the rest of the house."

There were no surprises. The rooms were large, the furniture a collection from several generations, some of it valuable, some not. All had been well cared for. Upstairs Kim pointed out her bedroom but kept the door firmly closed. At the other end of the hall she said, "You can take whichever room you want." Keeping her voice matter-of-fact, she said, "There's only one bathroom up here, so we'll have to share."

Matt nodded and chose the room with the largest bed. He set his suitcase next to the dresser. "Do you need help with your things?"

"No thanks." She didn't come into the room. "Why don't you get settled and meet me downstairs in a few minutes? I'll throw something together and we'll have a quick dinner."

Later, sitting on the sofa next to Kim, Matt reached for the coffeepot on the small table and refilled their mugs.

Kim smiled. "Thanks. Well, now that you've seen the whole house, do you still think we're doing the right thing with the restaurant?"

Matt took a swallow of coffee. "More than ever." He watched Kim absently fiddle with her mug, frowning at the steaming coffee. "Why don't you read her letter?" he suggested gently. "Maybe you'll feel better."

A rueful look crossed her face. "Sorry. Was I brooding?"

"A little." He picked up her tote from the floor beside the couch and handed it to her. "Read it."

Kim pulled out the letter and ripped open the envelope. She scanned the letter quickly, then reread it more slowly. "Oh, damn." Her voice was choked and she rummaged through her bag until she found some tissues. She wiped her eyes and blew her nose, then dabbed at her eyes again.

"Are you all right?"

"Yes. No." Her small smile wobbled at the concern in his voice. She shook her head. "Don't. Please."

Matt's instinct was to pull her into his arms. Instead he asked, "Don't what?"

"Don't offer me any sympathy. When I get like this, it's the worst thing you can do." She stood up, waving for him to stay seated. "I need a drink of water," she lied, dropping the letter in his lap. "Here, you can read it."

Matt accepted the feeble excuse, watching her straight back until she disappeared behind the swinging door. Then he picked up the letter.

My dearest Kim,

When you receive this letter, I will be gone. The going is long overdue. In fact, I am rather impatient with the whole process. There is a certain lack of efficiency that I deplore.

However, that is neither here nor there. I have asked your aunts to attend to certain matters for me, and they assure me that they will do so. To avoid further complications, I have turned other matters over to that young twerp, Orin Esmond. He may be dull as ditch water, but I hear that he is a good attorney.

I have told him about our arrangements—yours and mine—concerning my belongings. He is to follow your directions implicitly. And in case you have forgotten or I did not make myself clear, I will restate my wishes.

My property, my home and my personal belongings are in your care. I would give them to you if I could, but in order to provide for Tonto properly, they must be sold. You may pay a fair price for them and keep everything. If there is nothing you want, you may turn the whole kit and caboodle over to the twerp for an estate sale.

Whatever you want, take. There is no right nor wrong in the matter. As I have no family, what is left will simply go before the vultures who sell such items at resale for an exorbitant profit.

You have an extraordinary amount of common sense, and even more important—compassion. If my belongings can be put to use where others will enjoy them, arrange it.

I leave the matter entirely in your hands.

Nadine Beaumont

Matt folded the letter and was replacing it in the envelope when Kim came back. She stood near the kitchen door, fighting a losing battle; her eyes were misty and her cheeks were damp with tears.

Matt tossed the letter aside and opened his arms. "Come here."

Eight

Matt caught her easily.

Burrowing her face in his neck, Kim realized she was not surprised. Matt did everything easily, with a minimum of fuss. She slid her arms around his neck, holding tight. When she gave a shuddering sigh, his grasp tightened.

Matt didn't offer platitudes or comforting words. He held her silently, running one of his big hands from her nape to her tailbone in a slow, soothing cadence. Bit by bit she melted against him, savoring the hard muscles beneath her and his controlled strength.

Hazily she considered the word. Yes, Matt was controlled. And patient. She had seen the hunger in his gaze, but some deeply feminine instinct within her had known that he was one tiger that wouldn't pounce. That wasn't his style. He would watch. And wait. And when the time was right . . .

Growing dizzy from the scent of him, a subtle blend of soap, shaving cream and man, Kim sighed and shifted her head to the hollow of his shoulder.

His hand tightened on the curve of her hip. "Better?"

She nodded, her eyes narrowing to contented slits when his fingers smoothed the fabric of her slacks over her bottom.

"Who's the young twerp?"

Kim grinned, testing his muscular shoulder with her fingertips. "A whippersnapper in his early sixties."

Matt's chest vibrated with his deep chuckle. "A good lawyer?"

"So I hear." She nodded again, listening to the rapid beat of his heart, smiling because he wasn't nearly as calm as he wanted her to think he was. As much to prove it to herself as to provoke, she ran her fingers down his chest, stopping near his belt buckle. His heart gave a leap.

"Kim?" There was both question and warning in his strained voice, but before she could respond to either, he leaned over and turned off the lamp.

The room wasn't entirely dark. Moonlight streamed in through the open blinds, allowing her to see the intense look Matt was giving her. He wanted to be sure, she realized with sudden clarity. She also realized that it was too late for questions or warnings. Somewhere, somehow, the decision had been made.

Perhaps it had been when he'd said "friend" to her aunts, his eyes telling her he wanted to be far more than that. Maybe it had been in Mom's, when he'd told her so explicitly what he wanted. Maybe in her room at the B and B, when he'd shown her exactly how hungry he was for her then left her to go to his own room.

Whenever, wherever, the decision had been made.

"Yes." Kim pulled his head down and brushed her lips against his. When she let him go, Matt exhaled sharply and surged to his feet, taking her with him. As usual, she thought approvingly, he did it easily and with a minimum of fuss.

"Are the doors locked?"

She smiled up at him. "Uh-hmm."

He strode to the stairs and started up them.

"Matt," she pointed out, "you're still carrying me."

"I know." There was a wealth of satisfaction in his voice. "Do you mind?"

"Not at all." She smiled up at him, her eyes gleaming with anticipation. "I feel like Scarlet O'Hara."

"I'm not Rhett Butler," he said bluntly.

"I should have on a long gown, flowing over your arm and trailing down the stairs," she decided, caught up in the romantic image. "Or maybe—"

"No." Without breaking his stride, he shifted her higher and touched her mouth with his. "You're perfect just as you are."

Her hand tightened on his shoulder when he reached the top of the stairs and turned toward his room. "Do you really think so?"

Startled by the uncertainty in her voice, Matt came to a sudden stop in front of her bedroom door. "Yes."

She blinked at the utter conviction in his voice.

"Have you changed your mind?" His arms tightened around her. "This is your last chance, honey. I'll hate like hell doing it, but if you say the word, I'll leave you here at your door."

Kim scowled up at him. "Did I say I was changing my mind?" she demanded. The man was *impossible!*

His grin was a blend of relief and outright hunger. "No, you didn't."

Kim remained silent until he set her on her feet beside his bed. No, she assured herself, she wasn't having second thoughts. Just a massive case of insecurity. She wanted to be perfect for him and knew with appalling clarity that she was not. When he turned on the small dresser lamp she looked around and grasped at the first straw she found. "I don't have a nightgown," she announced casually. "I'll just go and—"

Matt caught her arm. "You don't need a gown," he said firmly. "You don't need a thing that you don't already have."

"It might help," she ventured. "I have this really slinky number that—"

"No." Matt slid his hands down and cupped her bottom, drawing her against him. His mouth closed over hers and he tasted coffee and the tantalizing sweetness of Kim's excitement.

"It's ecru," she murmured. "With lace."

"No." His lips touched her throat and he smiled against her skin when she shivered.

"And silky."

Matt tugged her blouse out of her slacks and spanned her waist with his hands. "So are you." When he looked down at her Kim's eyes widened.

"It's one of those things you've got to see to appreciate," she said rapidly. "Maybe I should just—"

Energy, Matt reminded himself. Kim was a woman who fairly shimmered with the stuff. Idleness made her uneasy; she was at her best under pressure, making things happen.

Matt reached for her hands. He placed a lingering kiss in each palm, then put them on the front of his shirt. "Help me."

"Do what?" she asked, diverted.

His grin was a wicked flash of white. "Take my clothes off."

After a surprised blink, Kim accepted the invitation with her usual zest. She unbuttoned the shirt and tugged it off his wide shoulders. Tossing it aside, she studied his chest. It, too, was wide, and liberally sprinkled with dark hair. Resting her palms just above his nipples, she worked her way down, coming to a stop when she reached the waistband of his jeans.

"Uh, Matt," she said slowly, "I think you ought to know that I've never done this before."

Matt was in the process of sliding her blouse back over her shoulders when he stopped, his hands pulling the fabric taut. Startled, he repeated, "You've never done this before? Why the hell didn't you tell me?"

"I *am* telling you," she said, warily eyeing a convulsive movement next to his zipper. "The subject just never came up. In the midst of a conversation, was I supposed to drop the fact that I've never undressed a man?"

"Is that what we're talking about? Undressing?"

Flustered, she scowled at him. "Aren't you listening to me?"

"With baited breath," he assured her.

"Yes, that's what we're talking about, and I just—"

"Kim," he asked carefully, "is there anything *else* you forgot to tell me?"

"—I just don't know how much delicacy is required for this part," she finished in a rush. "What do you mean, anything else?" she asked absently, focusing her attention on his waistband. "Like what?"

Matt took a deep breath. "God only knows," he muttered. Then he grinned at her look of utter concentration. She finally opened the button with a tentative nudge.

"You've got good instincts," he encouraged with another grin. "Use 'em."

Kim eased the zipper down with an excruciating caution. Her small hands were all over him, her fingers tracing the barrier beneath the fabric. Finally, assured that she was beyond the major obstruction, she gave a quick tug and pulled the zipper all the way down.

He inhaled sharply. *"Easy!"*

"What?" Kim slid her hands inside his jeans, shaping his lean buttocks with her palms. Matt stiffened, hardly breathing, his hands still tangled in her blouse. "You're falling behind," she pointed out politely.

With a suddenness that startled her Matt released her shoulders, stepped back and tore off the rest of his clothes, leaving them scattered where they fell. Then he turned his attention to her.

Kim drew a shaky breath. Matt was a man who wore clothes well; he wore nothing even better. Crisp dark hair covered his powerfully muscled chest, arrowed down to a narrow line that widened again low on his flat belly. He was beautifully, unabashedly male. He was also magnificently aroused.

"Now you." His silvery eyes caressed her as surely as his large, gentle hands.

Insecurity struck again when he eased her out of her blouse. Breasts too small, hips too big, thighs too soft—the litany of inadequacies rang in her head. "Wouldn't it be more romantic without the light?" she murmured as he released the silver belt buckle and smoothed her pleated slacks down to her ankles. She braced her hand on his shoulder when he knelt before her to finish removing them.

He grinned up at her, his gaze dropping to linger on her graceful, feminine curves. The silky scraps of fabric at her hips and breasts were more tantalizing than concealing. "More romantic than what?"

The sight of her worried face sobered him. He flowed to his feet and wrapped his arms around her, bringing her against his warmth. "Sweetheart, don't you know how beautiful you are?" Her lips touched his throat, and her dark red hair slid against his arm when she shook her head.

He tilted up her chin and looked into uncertain green eyes. "You're exquisite," he said deliberately. "How can you look at me, at my reaction to you, and doubt that?" He took her small hand in his and slid it down his chest, down his flat stomach. He curled her fingers around him.

"How can you touch me and doubt?" he muttered. "You turn me to fire with just a look, a smile." He released the front catch of her bra and eased the straps from her shoulders. Then he brushed his thumbs across the beaded tips of her breasts, satisfaction gleaming in his eyes when she gasped. With the same deliberation he hooked a finger on either side of her silky briefs and gave a sharp tug. He tossed them aside, cupping the lush curve of her bottom, pulling her closer.

"Look at me, Kim." His voice was strained. "Can you doubt the beauty that I see when I look at you?"

Kim stared up at his taut face. Pleasure was evident in his silvery eyes. So was hunger. So was approval beyond her dreams. Never had she been so affirmed by a single glance. Never had she been so tempted by a man. Never had she ached so for the touch of that one man.

She shook her head slowly. "No," she whispered. "I can't."

He closed his eyes, but not before she saw the relief that darkened them. When he opened them he said, "The day you walked into my office I began dreaming of this night. Dreaming of your hair fanned on the pillow beside me, of your face lighting up when we made love. Of watching you turn to silver in my arms—seeing in your eyes the knowledge that you have been well and truly loved. I ache with that need, Kim."

He tangled his hands in her hair and leaned down to kiss her. "But if your need is greater than mine, we'll turn out the lights." When sudden comprehension gleamed in her eyes he said simply, "It's your choice, honey."

Kim's smile was dazzling. She shook her head slowly. "Leave them on."

With an exultant grin Matt picked her up and held her tight against him in a fierce hug, then fell onto the bed with her. Rolling onto his back, he brought Kim with him, helping her sit up, holding her until she regained her balance.

Her eyes brightened with a blend of intrigue and fascination. She sat up straighter, her hands braced on his chest, her knees easing down beside his thighs. She gave a tentative jiggle. "I've never done this before, either," she confided with a small grin.

"A night of firsts," he said lazily, reaching up to smooth her hair over her breasts. "Do your worst."

"Has this been part of your fantasy, too?"

"Definitely."

"Interesting dreams you have, Mr. Kingsley."

"They've perked up considerably in the past few weeks, Ms. Cassidy." His eyes darkened and his smile faded. "Kiss me, Kim."

Answering the longing in his rough voice, she braced her hands on either side of his head and leaned forward, excitement sizzling through her like wildfire. Matt's groan of pleasure fanned the flames.

His hands tangled in her hair and he gently tugged her closer, groaning again when her breasts grazed his chest.

"You feel as good as I dreamed you would," he muttered, bringing her mouth to his. "Taste as good, too." He cupped her head in his hand, holding her there against him. "Better."

Kim ran her fingertips over his shoulders, skimming the strong rapid pulse that beat in his throat, his chin. Her mouth followed the same trail, touching, teasing, tempting, until Matt's hands dropped to her waist and he lifted her higher and stroked her beaded nipple with the tip of his tongue.

Her back arched and she gave a gasp of pure pleasure. His eyes shone up at her, a flash of silver through dark lashes and she held her breath, waiting for his touch. "You make me feel beautiful." The words were a breathless murmur.

"You are." He groaned when her hair slid across his chest like a banner of dark silk. "And sexy as hell."

"I know." The words were a soft purr. And she did. Now. Because of Matt every cell in her body sang with a feminine joy, exulted in the age-old dance of life. She leaned closer, needing his heat, the touch of his hands and mouth. "Touch me, Matt."

His tongue gently rasped her other nipple. "Like this."

"Yes."

Brushing his lips down the silky path between her breasts, he muttered, "And this?"

She shuddered. "Yes." Her restless fingers kneaded the hard muscles of his chest, tangling feverishly in the springy dark hair that covered it. *"Yesss!"*

Her broken cry and eager hands told Matt more than she knew. She needed him as much as he needed her. She was as hungry as he was. As ready as he was. And if he was not mistaken, Kim was about to experience another first. With him. Only with him. Savage exultation filled him at the thought.

With a sudden movement he rolled her onto her back, leaning over her. Kim reached for him, shifting restlessly. "I want you. All of you."

"You have me, sweetheart." His mouth lingered at her breast then moved down to the soft curve of her stomach. Then lower. Kim gasped, stilling as unutterable tension filled her.

"Matt?"

His lips curved in a smile against the soft flesh of her inner thigh.

"Oh, Matt!"

"Hmm?"

"I didn't know..."

"I know."

"Ah." Kim's voice was urgent in the darkness. "Now. Now. Now."

"Soon." His hands promised. His mouth drove her wild.

"Matt!" Kim's breath caught deep in her throat.

"What?"

"Help me!"

Dropping a final kiss on her soft belly, Matt surged up, bracing his forearms on either side of her head. He took a shuddering breath and reached for a small packet on the table, dropping a kiss on her sweat-dampened shoulder when she made a soft bereft sound. When he turned back to Kim her long legs wrapped around him, holding him closer, tighter. Meeting her dazed, demanding eyes with his own, he sheathed himself in her softness.

Kim convulsed around him, arching, clinging to him, rigid, shuddering with wave after wave of molten pleasure. Then he gave in to his own shattering release.

Much later he tightened his arms around Kim's waist, tugging her closer. She snuggled against him.

"Matt?" Her voice was drowsy.

"Mmm."

"It was . . ." She sighed. For once she was at a loss for words.

"I know." He kissed her bare shoulder. "A night of firsts. For me, too."

Kim stretched languidly, replete with contentment. The night had not been restful but it had been . . . very satisfying. Her outstretched arm brushed Matt's shoulder and she looked up into alert gray eyes.

"You're smiling," he said.

He looked relieved, she realized with surprise. "Did you expect me to take one look at you and run screaming from the room?"

He gathered her close, selecting his words carefully. "I was afraid things might look different to you this morning."

"They do," she assured him. "They look even better than they did last night." Looking out the window, she asked, "What time do you think it is? We're invited to the aunts' for breakfast."

"I remember." He reached out a long arm and lifted his watch from the table. "We have plenty of time." His dark brows lifted. "I thought you said they didn't like to cook."

Kim grinned. "They don't. And when they do they're awful. You tasted their cookies yesterday, remember?"

Matt grimaced.

"But they consider it their moral duty to provide me with at least one meal when I'm here. We all endure, and over the years we've found that their breakfasts are the least lethal."

Planting a kiss on her shoulder, Matt murmured, "At least they won't have to sneak me any magnolia tea. Or ginseng or orchid or whatever the hell that other one was."

Kim shot up, turning to face him. The covers pooled around her hips. "You *knew?*"

He grinned, trying to keep his eyes on her outraged face. "I looked in one of your herb books last night while you were fixing dinner. Aphrodisiacs are a fascinating subject."

"They really aren't, you know." She sighed. "Aren't aphrodisiacs, I mean. I just try to keep the aunts on the straight and narrow. Sometimes it's a losing proposition." Throwing back the covers she gave him a lingering glance that had an immediate effect on him. She said, "We'd better get moving."

"Kim."

The quiet word stopped her where she was, with one foot on the floor, the other bent beneath her. Something in his face made her move away from the bed, prompted her to say, "Did I miss something? Should I have asked if things look different to *you* this morning?"

"No, damn it, you shouldn't." His voice was rough, the expression in his eyes falling somewhere between anger and frustration. Or guilt, or regret. She couldn't tell.

"Then what's the matter?"

"I have to tell you something, and I don't want you to misunderstand."

"Oh, God." She looked for something to wrap around herself and finally settled on Matt's shirt. "You're married, right? A little detail you just forgot to tell me?"

"Married?" Matt blinked at the self-disgust in her voice, watching as she fumbled with the buttons.

Kim stared out of the window, rolling the sleeves up to her wrists. "With six kids waiting for Daddy to come home, no doubt. That's great, Kingsley. Just great."

"Kim, for God's sake, I'm not married, and I don't have any kids. Will you listen—"

She took another deep breath. "The IRS," she said in a voice of doom. "You haven't paid your taxes and they're going to put you away for the next ninety years."

"Damn it," Matt roared, "will you listen to me?"

"Well, *say* something," she yelled back. "Don't just keep telling me you're going to tell me. *Tell* me."

"Come here." He extended his hand. Kim looked at it doubtfully. "Please." When she came back and tucked her hand in his, he dropped a kiss in her palm and folded her fingers around it. Patting the bed he said, "Sit with me."

Kim sat, leaning back against the headboard. Drawing her legs up to her chest, she wrapped her arms around them and rested her chin on her knees. "I'm listening," she said quietly.

Matt raked his hand through his dark hair, wondering where to start.

"From the beginning," she prompted.

"Before we go out to the Beaumont place, I want to tell you about something I've been working on for several years."

Kim blinked. Business? After the night they had spent together, he wanted to talk about a hotel? She had geared herself up for an emotional free-for-all and he wanted to discuss a new project?

"Kim?" He touched her ankle. "Are you listening?"

She nodded. "With baited breath."

He frowned. "For several years I've been looking for a site for something special. The location is . . . crucial to its success."

When he paused Kim closed her eyes. "I don't think I want to hear this."

His hand smoothed her hair. "Just listen. Please."

Kim's lashes lifted a fraction. "You're not going to turn Posy Creek into some high tech entertainment center."

"You're absolutely right. That's the last thing in the world I'd do. I want to build a small, intimate retreat for stressed-out executives. Not a high rise, not a sprawling glass structure. Cottages spread out in the hills, far enough from each other to maintain an air of solitude. I want the people who stay there to hear the wind in the trees, the birds singing; to be able to sit on their porches and listen to the crickets."

"And you think that the Beaumont place might be what you're looking for?" she said slowly.

He nodded, unable to read her expression. "If it's like the rest of the area. Posy Creek is perfect."

"I know it's perfect, and I intend to keep it that way. How many cottages?"

He shrugged. "Depends on how much property there is. Ten, maybe fifteen. No more than that. In addition, there would be a main lodge and a restaurant."

"And how many people would the lodge accommodate?"

"None," he said firmly. "There will be a library, a game room and a bar. Just a place for the guests to socialize if they choose to."

"And what will keep the area from being congested with traffic?"

"We install a heliport at the far end of the property. We bring the guests in and out, staying away from the other houses and the town. We'll have a few cars available for guests who want to do some shopping." He eyed her thoughtful expression warily. "What do you think?"

"I think you've got this planned down to the last detail."

"I told you, I've been working on the idea for several years. But that's not what I meant, and you know it. What do you think?" he repeated.

Kim stared down at her toes. "I don't know. It all depends on who's running the thing and how committed he or she is to the environment and the community. It could be good or it could be a disaster."

"It's my baby, Kim." When she didn't look at him, his face hardened. "I'd be tougher on environmental issues than most of the residents. Not only because of the town itself, but because the whole reason for coming here would be for the quiet charm and the rural atmosphere. I realize that there will be zoning laws and that I'd need the approval of the town council. But before we get to any of that, I need to know how you feel."

"Maybe it could work," she said slowly. "At least, as long as you own it, as long as you retain control."

"I told you, it's my baby. I wouldn't sell it."

She raised her eyes to him, studying his face. What she saw there seemed to satisfy her. "We've all been worried about the property," she said slowly. "Afraid that developers would come in and build some atrocity. This could just be the answer to our problem. Maybe."

Swinging her feet to the floor, she said vaguely, "We'd better get ready now. Let me think about it. I'll use the shower downstairs."

It could have been a lot worse, Matt decided as he stepped into the shower. She could have told him to clear out. At least he had been spared that. So far. He lathered his chest with a herb-scented bar of soap, frowning.

She had taken it too quietly, he realized uneasily. He had grown accustomed to her enthusiasm, a spate of words that eventually fell into place and made perfect sense. He didn't know how to handle her silence.

He was in his jeans, hunkering down in front of the bathroom mirror when Kim came in. She looked like spring in yellow slacks and a matching top, and she was carrying a stool.

"Here." She set it down in front of the basin. "The mirror's too low for you."

"Thanks." He perched on the stool and was reaching for the can of shaving cream when he saw her reflection in the mirror. Their reflection.

Kim was looking at him, a pensive expression on her face. She pressed against him, resting her hands on his shoulders, touching, stroking with the tips of her fingers.

"Kim? Sweetheart, what's the matter?"

She slid one hand down on his chest, fingers gently kneading the hair-roughened surface. Then she looked up, meeting his eyes in the mirror. She shook her head. "Nothing. I don't know. Maybe everything."

Matt reached for her hands and pressed them to his chest, holding them there, feeling the beat of his heart through them. His voice was urgent. "Kim, this plan of mine for the Beaumont property has nothing to do with us. No more than the restaurant does. If it works, okay. If it doesn't—" he shrugged "—that's okay, too. One way or another, it won't affect us."

Her eyes evaded his. "Sure."

"Damn it, I mean it." He squeezed her hands. "Look at me, honey."

Troubled green eyes met determined gray ones.

Kim broke first. Blinking, she tugged at her hands. When he released them she touched his cheek in a fleeting gesture. "You'd better hurry, or we'll be late."

Nine

"Need any of these?" Kim pulled a bottle of antacid pills from the cupboard and held it up for Matt to see. He glanced up from drying the last plate and gave a wry shake of his head.

Watching him, the corners of Kim's mouth quirked in a small, very feminine smile of contentment, knowing that the question she had posed that first evening at her place had finally been answered. Matt *did* treat a woman with that same rapt, narrow-eyed concentration. And the woman in question was indeed lucky.

His warm gaze lingered on her mouth before lifting to meet her eyes. "You were right," he admitted, nodding toward the two old women chatting in the other room. "The meal was lethal."

Kim nodded. "If there's one thing I don't joke about, it's food," she reminded him. "Why do you think I learned to cook? It was a pure case of self-defense." She finished wiping the counter and looked up at him. "Are you through? Good. Let's visit with the aunts for a while before we drive out to the Beaumont place."

Matt felt a surge of hunger that had nothing at all to do with food and everything to do with Kim. He hadn't reacted to a woman like this in years. He dropped the towel and wrapped his arms around her, fitting her to the length of his hard body. Who was he kidding? He had *never* felt like this. With Kim, even a look of casual inquiry could knock him to his knees. With Kim, everything was different.

"I've got a better idea," he muttered urgently. "Let's go back to the house."

She nuzzled her cheek against his chest and made a small encouraging sound.

"Kim?" Valerian called from the other room. "Are you working that boy to death in there? What's taking you so long?"

When Matt groaned Kim stood on tiptoe to kiss him. "Later." Promise gleamed in her green eyes.

He kept her right where she was, where she belonged— so close he could feel her heartbeat. "How much later?"

"Kim? Matt?" Primrose called.

Kim's hands inched down from his shoulders to his waist. "Not one second later than it has to be."

The aunts' whispered conversation broke off abruptly when Matt and Kim joined them. They glanced from one to the other and exchanged a look of deep satisfaction.

"You two look very happy," Primrose observed, her eyes bright with interest.

"It's a very lovely morning," Kim said sedately.

"Lovely," Matt echoed, looking down at her glowing face, touching her cheek in a fleeting gesture with the back of his fingers.

The two women raised their brows in silent communication. They sat at a game table almost hidden by a stack of newspapers—thick, colorful, Sunday editions. Primrose was extracting one small section from each paper, carefully stacking the remaining pages in another pile.

"Want to read one?" Valerian offered, looking at Matt. "You can have your choice. They range from San Diego to Seattle."

Kim took a chair near her aunts, watching Matt, a trace of amusement lurking in her eyes.

He eyed the pile of papers thoughtfully, then shook his head. "Thanks, but I'd rather see the one from Posy Creek."

"There's no such animal," Primrose told him, setting aside another supplement. "Not much happens out here. Besides, Miller's market is faster."

"When something newsworthy happens around here, everyone calls Miller's," Valerian explained, taking pity on Matt's confused expression. "Then we all find out about it when we do our grocery shopping."

Judging by their animated expressions, marketing was given a high priority in Posy Creek. He could see why. Joining them at the table, he nodded at the stack of papers. "Why so many?"

Primrose sighed. "It's a terrible waste, but they won't send us just the obituaries. They say we have to order the whole thing."

"Terrible waste," Valerian echoed, watching her sister detach the supplement from the last paper. "We told them that we didn't want any more trees cut down on our account—especially since we never read the other sections—but no one will sell just part of a paper."

Primrose brushed back her orange hair and jabbed a pointy-toothed comb in it. "The news never changes," she explained. "And it's depressing. Countries that were fighting years ago are still fighting. Politicians still argue, and people get mugged in the cities."

Matt looked from one to the other. "And reading obituaries cheers you up?"

Their eyes brightened.

"Matt?" A ripple of laughter warmed Kim's voice. "I think you might be interested in this." She held up a slim booklet that had obviously seen better days. It was dog-eared and stained and held together with large paper clips and tape.

"It's about Posy Creek," she told him, waiting while he moved his chair next to hers. "It must be at least twenty years old, but the information is pretty much the same." She flipped through the pages and stopped at the middle. "This is what I wanted you to see."

Matt glanced down, his eyes narrowing when he realized that he was looking at a map of the property lines in the area. "This is still the same, too?"

Kim nodded. "Families around here don't sell, they pass their land on. See the area stretching between here and town?" She tapped the page with a slim finger. "That's our herb farm."

"Someday it will all belong to Kim," Primrose said, busily scanning the latest crop of obituaries from Los Angeles. She made an annoyed clucking sound. "Valerian, look at this. Three more notices asking people to donate money to a charity instead of sending flowers! What is this world coming to?"

Kim nudged Matt with her elbow. "One end of the Beaumont place borders ours. Along here." She pointed again, and he nodded.

"Never mind," Valerian soothed. "We'll take care of it. After all, a body should have *some* flowers around to send them on their way."

"And this end of Mrs. Beaumont's butts up to the mountain." Kim's finger traced a path on the paper.

Primrose frowned and took a last look at the names listed. "I don't see that actor's grandma in here. Poor old lady's been hanging on by a frayed thread. Do you suppose—"

Valerian reached over and patted her hand. "We'll start listening to the news. Something's bound to happen soon."

Anticipation fairly quivered in Primrose's voice. "They say Monty Murphy's a real stickler for keeping his family out of the limelight. More than likely it'll be a private service."

"I know." Valerian's smug smile made Matt blink. "Bristling with security."

Primrose neatly folded the paper. "Do you think I should call Barney and mention that we might be taking a trip?"

"He always manages to get us tickets, but I suppose it wouldn't hurt." While her sister trotted out of the room, Valerian turned to Kim. "I think I've misplaced Theo's itinerary. Exactly where is he now?"

Kim grinned. "Probably somewhere between Tampa and Chicago. Too far away to interfere."

"Good." Valerian smiled again and trailed after her sister.

Matt watched her hasten across the room, then turned his sharpened gaze on Kim. "Just what are they up to?" he demanded.

"You sound just like Uncle Theo," she said with a grin. "What makes you think they're up to anything?"

"I can smell it," he said flatly. "Tell me."

Why was it that men always felt they had to straighten out the women in their lives? Kim wondered, studying Matt's stubborn chin. With a shrug, she concluded that it must be genetic.

"It's nothing that requires any heavy-handed male interference," she told him. "It's just their...hobby."

"Hobby." He considered the word. "What is?"

Kim's voice broke on a soft gurgle of mirth. "Breaking into private funerals."

"Of people they don't know?" His voice rose on the last word.

"Of course! It's no fun going to a funeral for someone you care about," she explained patiently. While he was still grappling with that she added, "It's the ones for the rich and famous that they really zero in on."

"Why, for God's sake?"

"Don't be thickheaded. Because they're harder to get into, of course. Usually, only family and close friends are invited, and there are security guards to keep out the masses."

"So what's the point?"

"I think it's the challenge—like climbing a mountain because it's there. Of course, Uncle Theo says they're just asking for trouble."

Matt looked like he agreed. "Sounds ghoulish to me."

Kim shook her head. "Not from their point of view. First of all, they only go if the, uh, deceased is very old. They figure that the...person has outlived most of his or her friends and could use a few more genuine mourners. And since my aunts are sentimental ladies, once they break through the security system, they truly do mourn. They stand there in their black dresses and furs and cry into their hankies, looking fragile and pathetic." She added thoughtfully, "They're probably more sincere than a lot of the mourners are."

Matt shook his head. "And they always send flowers."

"Of course!" Valerian trotted back into the room, her arms full of what looked like dried branches. When she placed them carefully on the table, Matt saw that they were heart-shaped wreaths with pink, starlike flowers entwined with bright yellow ones. "*Sedum purpureum* and *Chelidonium majus*," she said proudly. "Most people call them live-forever and celandine. In the language of flowers, which covers every situation imaginable, celandine means joys to come. Live-forever is quite obvious."

Matt walked over and looked down at the flowers, then at the small woman fussing with them. "That's your own personal...metaphysical message?"

Valerian looked up, pleased. "Exactly. When Primrose and I send flowers to people—live people, that is—we select them very carefully because the message is there whether the recipient understands it or not. It's a responsibility." Sighing, she added, "Some people think we have no right to mix flowers and messages—"

"Uncle Theo, primarily," Kim interjected.

"—that it's a form of meddling." She blinked indignantly. "But it's no such thing."

Matt touched one of the wreaths. "So, basically, you have your own fragrant telegram service."

Primrose bustled in as her sister nodded. "Barney said just call when we're ready. He'll get us on a plane." She picked up the paper again. "We'd better decide who we're sending these to and call the messenger service."

The two women were still hunched over the obituaries and flowers when Matt and Kim said their goodbyes.

Matt stuffed the remaining food in the basket before he leaned back against the broad tree trunk and watched Kim tidily store the paper napkins. By now, he reflected, he should be used to the primitive surge of possession that filled him whenever he was with her...or saw her...or thought of her. He should be, but he wasn't. The raw emotion still stunned him.

She was wearing a tormenting smile and was semidecently covered by pink shorts and a matching sleeveless top. From the top of her shiny, mussed hair down to her bare toes, she looked happy. And tempting. And like she had a delicious secret.

He held out his hand and waited until her fingers touched his. "Come here."

Kim went. Willingly. Gladly. Savoring the hunger in his eyes. She rested her head in the hollow of his shoulder and slowly unbuttoned his shirt, smiling when he uttered a dark, encouraging sound.

She couldn't have ordered a more perfect day, she reflected, lazily threading her fingers through the dark springy hair on his chest. All the necessary ingredients were there: Matt, sunshine, a soft, scented breeze and Posy Creek. They were in her favorite retreat—a small glen in the far corner of her property, blanketed in wildflowers, completely encircled by live oaks. Through some fluke of nature, the tree against which they leaned curved parallel to the ground rather than reaching upward. It had always been a magical place for her, a place where she brought her dreams, her hopes. Today she had brought Matt.

He covered her hand with his. "Nice."

"What's nice?"

"You."

She tilted her face toward him and smiled. "Thank you."

"And this place."

Prodding at his chest with a slim finger, she said, "A little more enthusiasm, if you please. This is a *wonderful* place. Magical, as a matter of fact."

Matt's brows rose. "Oh?"

"I think I detect a bit of skepticism. Come on." She jumped to her feet and held out her hand. "I'll show you." She scooped up the blanket and tossed it to him, then led him through a canopy of oaks. Finally she stopped and said, "You have to close your eyes. Don't open them until I say the magic word." He obediently lowered his lids, moving when she tugged at his hand, feeling the sun touch his face, then deep, cooling shade.

Kim stopped. "One, two, three, abracadabra!"

Matt opened his eyes. "You're right," he said, his intent gaze never leaving her vivid face. "You're magic."

"I don't mean me." But she smiled. Waving to the small oasis before them, she pointed to the spot where a narrow stream meandered through the trees and trickled into a small pool. "That's it."

"Magic, huh?"

"Definitely. Elves and unicorns come here when there's no one else around." She took the blanket from him and dropped it at their feet. "And there's a mystical quality to time," she informed him. "There is no yesterday, no tomorrow. And later," she said precisely, emphasizing the word as she slid her hands beneath his open shirt and eased it over his shoulders, "is right now."

Matt dropped a swift kiss on her upturned lips and stepped back to shrug out of his shirt. Kim pulled hers over her head and dropped it along with the rest of her clothes on the blanket. Within seconds they were wading into the waist-deep pool.

Kim shuddered as the water splashed up on her. "I forgot how cold it is. I'm freezing!"

Matt steadied her, watching the silvery ribbons of water trickle over her taut breasts. "No," he said simply, "you're beautiful." He watched as one sparkling drop worked its way down and clung to the tight bead of her nipple, trembling and glittering in the sunlight. With a hoarse mutter he dropped his hands to her waist and lifted her high against him. Kim's murmur was both hungry and encouraging, and when his tongue captured and savored the droplet of water, she convulsively wound her arms around his neck, holding him close.

"Don't let me go." It was a whisper, a plea, a promise.

"I couldn't." His mouth traced a path to her other breast. "Come closer."

Shivering, she wrapped her legs around his waist.

"Closer."

Kim's arms tightened in a demand of her own, and time passed in shimmering sensations as she trailed her fingers down his back, touching, stroking and arching against him. Finally, slowly, she slid down his hard frame into the pool that seemed to have absorbed the warmth from the rising heat of their bodies.

Scooping water in her cupped hands, she raised it high, like a priestess with an ancient offering, then parted her fingers and let it trickle down his chest. She followed it with her hands, stroking the water over his shoulders, smoothing it through the dark hair that covered his chest, down his flat stomach. Down, down until it joined the water lapping at the juncture of his thighs.

Matt made a muffled sound and with a quick movement lifted her into his arms. "Let's go, sweetheart."

Kim blinked up at his taut face. "Where?"

"Where I can hold you against me without worrying that you might slip downstream," he said bluntly, heading for dry ground. "Where I can touch you and love you properly." He placed her gently on the blanket and dropped down beside her, making a contented sound deep in his throat when she pressed her water-cooled body against him.

"Kiss me, Kim." She did, reaching up to him with a need that matched his own, and he took her mouth in a long soaring kiss that went on forever and left her limp and breathless against him. His arms tightened reflexively around her slender waist, tugging her even closer.

The kiss wiped away all humor, all teasing, and left them clinging with a hunger and passion that dazed them. It had been building for weeks, fed by their close contact and the tension that vibrated between them. Making love the night before hadn't really eased the situation; it had merely brought their need further into the open.

His mouth slanted over hers in a kiss that deepened in an instant, drowning them both in a haze of heat. "I need you, Kim."

Her senses responded to the harsh whisper, tightening her fingers in his thick hair. Slowly, so slowly, his hand covered her breast, lingered lovingly then drifted down, exploring, touching, tempting.

"Oh, Matt!" Her shaken whisper was a silken goad, urging him on.

"Touch me, sweetheart. Take me in those soft little hands of yours." When she reached for him, he gasped, "Yes, oh God, *yes!*" His mouth fastened hungrily on hers and he savored her sleek body, felt her damp warmth and knew with exultation that she wanted him now—needed him now—as much as he needed her.

Her body arched when he sheathed himself in her welcoming softness, her breathless cry a sound of pure pleasure. Heat and power, rhythm and wild joy. She tightened around him as small tremors began deep within her. They grew, radiated outward, touching him, wrapping around him.

Shaken to his core, Matt whispered, "Mine. You're mine. Mine, mine . . . *Kim!*"

Her eyes met his in a look that seared his soul, and she cried out as they shuddered together in perfect release.

Much later Matt turned his head and looked at Kim. She was lying beside him, gazing through the curtain of leaves to the cloudless sky above, her expression lazy and contented.

"I still don't understand why the aunts need all of those newspapers," he said, knowing exactly what her reaction would be. "Aren't there enough sick people around here?" He was right, he reflected with satisfaction. She turned to him, a half grin of love and amusement lighting her face.

"You're missing the whole point," she told him.

He touched her cheek with a gentle hand. "And that is?"

"There's just no scope for their talents around here. Local funerals are open to everyone." She dropped a quick kiss on the strong pulse beating in his neck. "It's just their way of keeping tabs on the West Coast—and ailing celebrities. They read all the death notices, decide where to send flowers and where to make a flying condolence call. At the drop of a casket lid they jump into their basic blacks, haul out their furs and take off. Of course, Uncle Theo predicts a bad end for them. He just knows he'll have to post bail for them someday."

Matt sat up and pulled her into his lap. "Don't you worry about them?"

"Why?" she asked simply. "Who in their right mind would set the dogs on two little old ladies crying pathetically into their hankies?" She shook her head. "No, I say let them have their fun and incidentally spread a little joy at some very sad occasions.''

"Hmm." Matt absently traced his thumb down her spine. "I suppose so."

Kim was close enough to feel his sudden tension, to see the flicker of darkness in his eyes, and knew precisely when he made the mental leap to another, more troubling, matter.

"Okay," she sighed. "Let's get this behind us. We've seen the house, looked at rooms chock-full of wonderful furniture and walked over Mrs. Beaumont's property. Now we've got to talk. Do you want the place or not?"

His arm tightened around her waist. "I might have known you'd leap right to the bottom line."

"Why not? That's where I always find you." She frowned at him. "Tell me straight out. Do you want it?"

"Yes."

Kim waited, her brows lifted. "That's it? Yes? No big sales pitch? Just yes?"

He sighed. "Okay, I want it. It's exactly what I've been looking for, and I don't know if I'll ever find anything else so perfect. How's that?"

Kim thought about it. "All right."

Matt wound a strand of her silky hair around his finger. "What does that mean? That I made a fair attempt at communicating?"

"No." She shook her head. "It means, all right, if I really have the authority to make the decision, you can have it."

Matt stared at her, stunned by the concession. He had been prepared for resistance, for anger, for anything but a simple yes.

"Damn it, Kim!" He dumped her off his lap onto the blanket. Surging to his feet, he scowled down at her. His frown grew darker when she smiled at him. "That's a hell of a way to do business! Sweetheart, you've got to toughen up. First of all, you're supposed to twist my arm for the highest price you can get."

"With certain provisions, of course," she murmured, crossing her legs Indian style.

He paced to the end of the blanket. "You know how bad I want it, so you dig in and make me pay through the nose!"

Kim held up her index finger. "First I and the town planning commission have to approve the plans."

Matt turned and stalked to the other corner, determined to teach her the basics of hardball. "You don't give in until I agree to pay a hell of a lot more than it's worth."

She held up three more fingers. "Part of the money will go to Tonto's perpetual care, and the rest in a trust fund. You can't sell the property to anyone at a later date. If you ever get rid of it, you have to return it to Posy Creek for the same amount you paid for it."

Matt perched on the tree trunk and continued his lecture on piranha tactics. "You tell me it will be impossible to get the approval of the planning commission without your support. That I need your expertise—and that I pay plenty for it."

Kim wiggled her thumb. "A small percent of the annual profits will be donated to the city for the library and school and the park."

"Then and *only* then do you think about signing a contract."

She started on the other hand. "And you pay whatever it costs for me to hire a lawyer as good as yours to fiddle with the contract."

Apparently her words finally got through to him. Matt ground to a halt and stared down at her. He had the astonished look of a man who had just been clawed by a purring kitten. *"What did you say?"*

Kim's lashes lowered, but not before he saw the satisfaction gleaming in her green eyes. "I think you heard me. But if you *did* miss any of it, I've got it all written down for you."

Driving back to the house, Matt took his eyes from the road to glare at her. "What makes you think I'm going to pay for your lawyer?"

Kim looked out of her window, a small smile playing over her lips. "Because I'm not asking an arm and a leg for the property," she pointed out in a reasonable voice.

"Hell, no! All you're asking for is an annual percent of the profits!"

"Just a small one." She let the fuming silence build then asked, "Who will you put in charge? Who can you trust to run the place exactly as you've planned? It would be a big change in life-style," she reminded him. "He or she would have to live in Posy Creek."

"I've got someone in mind."

Her eyes widened. "Already? Who?"

"Me."

"You?"

Kim couldn't have sounded more shocked if he had announced that he planned to accompany her aunts buck naked on their next undercover venture.

Matt tightened his grip on the steering wheel. "I've thought about it," he admitted cautiously.

"Living here? You're kidding." Kim smiled, waiting for the punch line. When it didn't come she turned to face him, studying his expressionless face. "You *are* kidding, right?"

"What if I'm not?"

"Then I'd say you're going through what a lot of people experience when they come here for a visit." Kim smoothed the strap of her seat belt then looked back at him. "It happens all the time, Matt. Believe me. And it lasts about forty-eight hours, max."

His brows rose and she sighed. "It's true. People come, kick back on the front porch, watch the clouds roll by, breathe the fresh air and decide it would be a great place to live. The next day they're asking directions to the nearest mall. The one after that they're packing the car and rolling out of town."

"Why?" he asked quietly.

"*Why?*" She waved a hand at the passing scenery. "Look around you. There's nothing out there, that's why. Most people need more in their lives than trees, birds and crickets. Lord knows, I love Posy Creek—I always have and I always will, but that doesn't mean I'm blind to its limitations. There's nothing to do here, Matt. You'd go crazy."

She swung her head around, her hair flying out in a fragrant cloud. "Why do you think I moved to San Francisco?" She didn't give him a chance to answer. "Because it's the most exciting city on the West Coast, that's why. It's got everything!"

Ten

Everything.

That night Matt turned on his side in Kim's bed—in the room that was like Kim herself: fragrant, enticing and feminine—and considered the word. That and one other. He tightened his arm around Kim's waist, his eyes tender when she sighed in her sleep and nestled her bottom in the cradle of his thighs.

His hand flattened on the soft swell of her stomach and he considered the reality of having everything, including a dream. Kim had left Posy Creek searching for hers, and ended up in his hometown. She was right, of course. San Francisco *was* bustling and energetic, electric. Brash and sophisticated. Its possibilities were limitless.

Kim had found her pot of gold at the end of the rainbow, practically under the Golden Gate Bridge. She had an apartment in a trendy part of town, was doing work she loved. When the new restaurant opened she'd be on top of the heap. It wouldn't take long for word to get around, and her face would be smiling out from the glossy pages of food magazines. She'd probably be doing spots on local talk shows. And she would love every minute of it. He grinned. She'd wave her arms, talk ninety miles an hour and sweep the whole city up in her enthusiasm.

But Kim had gotten more then she'd bargained for when she'd moved to the coast, he reflected. Now she was involved with a man who was an integral part of the city, a product of San Francisco. A man whose family had deep roots there, both in the social and business arenas. A man—at least, according to those who seemed to know—who was the epitome of San Francisco life: an elegant, urbane shark. His smile grew cynical. A man who had it all. Everything.

A man who wanted to move to Posy Creek.

He wondered fleetingly how much his background had to do with Kim's willingness to become involved with him. Not his money; he knew her better than that. But his involvement, his permanence in "Baghdad by the Bay" might be part of the attraction. Because as far as he could tell, living in a metropolitan area was an essential part of her dream, and he was the one man she could expect to remain precisely where he was—in the middle of the city.

And what about *his* dream? What about Posy Creek?

Matt knew himself well enough to know that the question had to be resolved. Examined and put to rest, once and for all.

All right, he asked himself wearily, what about Posy Creek?

He liked everything about it—the quiet, the fragrance in the soft air, the slow pace. He grinned. Even the aunts, who were as crazy as bedbugs but darlings all the same. Liked? Hell, he wanted to stay with a fierceness that stunned him. And he had a strong feeling that the old ladies knew it, that his enthusiasm had given away more than he'd intended. He had caught their exchanged glances of delight when he'd discussed the project.

He would give his right arm to stay.

But he wouldn't give Kim.

And ultimately, that's what it would boil down to. The price of his dream would be the glow of excitement in Kim's eyes, the enthusiasm that she wore like a banner. And nothing was worth that. Not one thing.

He cupped her breast in his hand, flexing his fingers, smiling when she murmured and snuggled closer.

What the hell, he reflected, he could still build the retreat. That hadn't changed. The property was still there—even if Kim was nailing his hide to the wall for it. And he would buy it all. The plans were still the same. What furniture in the Beaumont house they didn't use for the restaurant could be divided among the cabins and the lodge. It was still a good idea.

Hell, it was still a *great* idea.

And there was no need for him to personally deal with all of the details. He didn't have to be on the site every day. Mary had been nagging him to start delegating some of his work. This might be the time to start.

When his arm tightened convulsively around Kim's waist at the thought, she stirred. "Matt?"

"Shh," he whispered soothingly, leaning down to brush a kiss on her shoulder. "Go back to sleep. Finish your dream. Everything's . . . all right."

Nothing was right anymore.

Kim dropped the new advertising campaign on the table with a small dissatisfied sound and stalked over to her tiny balcony, stepping outside to view what she could of the city below.

Gazing at the distant blue-green water, her mind drifted over the last two weeks since she and Matt had returned from Posy Creek. They had finally managed to select a name for the restaurant—The Turret. Business was going on as usual.

And she had spent most of the nights with Matt at the hotel.

She had told Margo where she would be, and the Trents were biting the bullet, trying to act like landlords instead of concerned friends.

Kim took a deep breath and exhaled slowly. All right, she admitted, she was stalling. She was in a state of shock, still recovering from the two bombshells Matt had dropped that morning. The first had come as they stepped out of the shower, after she had entertained herself by sculpting whorls of lather on his chest and flat stomach. He had draped a thick towel over her shoulders and casually mentioned an astronomical figure for the advertising campaign. The enormity of her commitment had hit her once again and was still weighing her down.

The next—and even more astounding—had come while they were eating breakfast. He had proposed.

Marriage.

Ensnared by the look of sated satisfaction in his smoky eyes, she had blinked and said, "What did you say?"

"Will you marry me?" He had repeated the words deliberately, reaching for her hand. "I want it all, Kim. You, a family, the works. Will you?"

"I don't know."

And that was the truth. She hadn't known then and she didn't know now. Leaning against the door frame, she reached down to rub a sprig of mint between her fingers, telling herself that she was crazy. Any normal red-blooded woman who had just received a proposal from a wonderful and handsome and sexy male—one who also happened to be rich and nice—should be leaping into the air and doing cartwheels.

So why wasn't she? Why was she standing here feeling depressed and...

Like a fraud?

Kim stiffened with shock at the uninvited question, her first impulse to deny it. But as with most thoughts that seemed to spring from nowhere, this one had apparently worked its way through layers of subconscious and was now demanding a fair hearing.

Fraud?

She shook her head. No way. She was working an honest twelve to fourteen hours a day trying to bring about the opening of The Turret on schedule. She was doing exactly what she had promised to do: give Matt a damn good restaurant. She was giving it everything she had, working until she was too exhausted to think, withholding nothing.

Except maybe...honesty?

Kim blinked thoughtfully. Scruples, she decided finally, were a pain in the neck. They nitpicked at unimportant details, totally overlooking the big picture. Besides, even if she was working now with less enthusiasm than she had begun with, it wasn't affecting the results. Things were still moving ahead of schedule.

Yes, there were problems, but she could cope. She was doing fine. Just fine.

Baloney.

Kim yanked at the sprig of mint and crunched it between her teeth. All right, maybe things weren't so fine. Maybe she shouldn't have gone home to Posy Creek.

Maybe she *was* homesick. Maybe the trip had brought out all of the feelings she'd been ignoring for the past few months. Maybe a lot of things. But the fact was: she had a promise to keep, a debt to pay. Matt had taken a chance on an unknown, and he was never going to regret it.

Because she was going to stay right here and keep her promise.

It wouldn't be so bad, she told herself bracingly. San Francisco was still the city she had fallen in love with. It still had majestic bridges, spacious parks, museums, the arts. It hadn't changed a bit. More important it had one other thing that Posy Creek would never have.

Matt.

And wherever Matt was she wanted to be. *Needed* to be.

He was a part of this big bustling city. He belonged here. She had known that before she'd even met him. She could never ask him to leave, or put him in a position where he was forced to choose between her and his home.

Nor would she play on the fact that he had seemed to like Posy Creek, had even—for a few seconds—toyed with the idea of moving there. Because even if her heart had skipped with hope, she had recognized the suggestion for what it was—the fleeting lapse of a man charmed by something new and different.

San Francisco couldn't be blamed if there were a few things it *didn't* have. Like family. Like a beautiful old home that had sheltered four generations of Cassidys. A market like Miller's where friends and neighbors gathered, and an old oak tree that had listened to the secrets of a little girl.

Kim shrugged, took a fortifying breath and turned back into the room to resume studying the advertising material. This time she vowed she would consider the merits of the project—not examine it from the viewpoint that the lavish amount of money invested was another link in the chain that kept her from going home.

However, the thought was still with her later that evening when she was sitting next to Matt on the large perfect sofa that was an integral part of his large perfect suite. She was tucked in the curve of his arm, her head on his shoulder. "I know what's wrong with this room," she said abruptly. "There's not a trace of you here. No family pictures, no knickknacks, nothing."

He ran a finger down her slim arm, a look of intense pleasure in his narrowed eyes when she shivered. "I use it to entertain a lot."

"So? I have people in my place, too, but I don't keep my things hidden."

"Your guests are friends. Mine are business associates."

She shook her head. "This place looks like a very expensive, very well kept museum."

"Want to redecorate?" He smiled down at her, touching a finger to her hair. "Say yes and you can bring all the plants and lace curtains you want."

"Sounds tempting." Her answering smile faded and her eyes grew dark. She turned to face him, reaching up to frame his face with her hands. "Very tempting," she whispered. When he bent his head and brushed his lips across hers, she slid her arms around his neck in a swift, reckless movement. "Matt?" Her voice was urgent. "Take me to bed? Love me?"

Wordlessly he slid one arm beneath her knees, the other behind her shoulders and carried her into the other room.

He was losing her.

Matt lay in the darkened room with his arm around Kim's waist, supporting her. She was asleep, half-sprawled on top of him. His arm tightened convulsively at the thought of losing her, and she muttered a protest, rubbing her cheek on his chest.

He contemplated the ceiling, stroking her back to soothe her. Something had happened while they were at Posy Creek—something other than his near slip about moving there to supervise the project. Kim had been different since their return.

He considered fatigue, then disregarded the notion; she had put in just as many hours before the trip. The difference now was that she didn't appear to be enjoying them. Her enthusiasm had dimmed and there was a vestige of strain in her beautiful eyes.

Ordinarily Kim made love the way she did everything else—with exuberance and zest, driving him crazy with her teasing. Tonight she had torn off her dress, shed the rest of her clothes and silently clung to him. He had tasted her desperation.

Matt filled his hand with her hair and carefully smoothed it down the elegant curve of her back. He'd find out what was bothering her, he promised himself, drawing the sheet over her shoulders.

And when he did, he'd fix it.

The next evening while Kim was brushing her hair, she heard Matt's voice in muted conversation in the other room. Then the door closed and he came back to the bedroom, shrugging into his jacket. She put down the brush and looked up at Matt's reflection in the mirror when he stopped behind her. "Who was that?"

His expression was thoughtful. "Messenger service. With flowers."

She tilted her head, studying the amusement in his eyes. "I'll take a wild guess." Her voice was resigned. "The aunts."

"Right." He touched a gentle finger to her hair. "How did they know you'd be here?"

Kim shrugged. "I stopped asking things like that a long time ago." After a moment's reflection she decided that she wasn't surprised. She had seen the thrilled look the two women had exchanged when she and Matt had arrived for breakfast that morning. The morning after she and Matt had officially changed status from boss and employee to boss, employee and lovers. And although the aunts had been tactful enough to remain silent, they had made it clear that they were delighted.

"I take it there's something...unusual about the flowers?"

He shrugged. "*I* don't recognize any of them. If they're sending a message I need a translation." He extended a hand. "Come and see."

When she tucked her small one in it he turned her around slowly. She wore a pale yellow sheath with a double row of matching buttons down the front. Matching linen shoes and a few gold chains completed the picture.

"Nice," he murmured. "But I like what's beneath it even better."

She grinned, more than satisfied with the masculine appreciation gleaming in his eyes. "Come on, let's go see those flowers."

Matt was right, she decided a moment later. They were different. There were two large baskets, one for each of them. Matt's was brimming with small white flowers, larger yellow ones and large weedy leaves. Her basket was a mass of poplar leaves, large white chrysanthemums, pansies and tiny greenish-white blossoms.

"So what do you think?" he asked.

Kim shook her head. "I don't know." She was staring at them thoughtfully when the phone rang.

"I'll get it." Matt lifted the receiver and listened, a surprised look crossing his face. "Hold on a minute." He turned to Kim with an apologetic shrug. "This may take a while."

"That's okay." She took a last look at the flowers and moved to the door. "I'll go on down and tell Claude to hold our table."

His brows lifted. "You think he'd give it to someone else?"

"I'm being tactful," she explained, resting her hand on the knob. "Take care of your call. I'll meet you downstairs." She blew him a kiss and closed the door behind her.

She could have stayed there, she reflected as she rode down in the silent elevator. Matt wouldn't have minded; in fact, he probably would have preferred it that way. So why hadn't she waited for him in the suite?

The only conclusion she had reached by the time she arrived at the main lobby was that it had to do with a sudden, unsettled feeling—and the feeling had something to do with the flowers. She wanted to think—and she wanted to be alone while she did it.

The aunts loved to send flowers, and when they did they usually thought they had a good reason. And that, she decided, stepping from the elevator, was what she wanted to mull over. Obviously a funeral was not involved, nor was there an anniversary. That left only a more subtle means of communication. And while Valerian and Primrose were often baffling and obscure, they were not known for their subtlety.

Kim delivered her message to the maître d' and wandered out to the main lobby where she found a comfortable chair hidden by the Kingsley's pricy version of a potted palm.

Sitting in the hotel lobby watching the foot-traffic was something that Kim found endlessly fascinating. There was a distinct sense of anticipation in the murmurs of the well-dressed clientele that was energizing, and the feeling was merely enhanced by observing the smooth efficiency of Matt's staff.

It was a place where Kim frequently came when she was mulling over a problem. The subdued bustle allowed her mind to wander while she examined miscellaneous bits of information. She knew that there was a purpose to the seemingly aimless mental drifting, and she no longer attempted to force the process. It had taken some doing, but she had finally gotten the message: this was the one area that would not respond to an impatient nudge.

Kim stayed in the comfortable chair until a large, happy party of convention goers took the seats around her. When their laughter grew too loud she moved. She was passing an area the staff called the rain forest, a luxuriant tangle of tropical ferns tucked discreetly between the elegant main lobby and one of the bars, when she heard the muffled cry of greeting.

"Kim! Pssst!"

Puzzled, she stopped by the solid wall of greenery and looked around.

"Kim!" The agitated cry came again.

"Aunt Valerian?" Astonished, Kim turned and studied the corridor behind her.

"Over here!"

"Here" seemed to be right in the heart of the man-made showpiece that was pampered by one of the hotel's florists. "Aunt Primrose?"

"Yesss!"

There was no doubt about it. The flustered hiss came from both of her aunts. It also came from the midst of the very high-priced display of ferns and other assorted flora. The display was not only costly and pampered, Kim recalled, it was normally scrutinized closely by hotel security.

Kim turned slowly, and even though she was expecting it, she was startled by the sight of two flushed faces peering out at her from behind the pinnate leaves of a baby Senegal palm.

"Is there anyone else out there?" Valerian waved a hand toward the lobby and lifted her voice to be heard over the waterfall. "Once we got in here, we were too embarrassed to come out."

"Shh!" Kim had learned that Matt's staff was very well trained, but it was still difficult to cope with the fact firsthand. Two tall, muscular young men were bearing down on her, moving at a pace that swiftly ate up the distance.

"Trouble, Kim?" They came to a stop beside her.

"Hi, Bill, Mark." She smiled up at them. "Uh, no, no trouble at all." She waved at the two women crouched behind the palm. "These ladies are my aunts and guests of Mr. Kingsley. They are also botanists," she lied, allowing her smile to grow brighter, "who got a little carried away. Will you help them out, please?"

When the two women were on solid ground again Kim looked at the clumps of loam scattered on the dove-gray carpet. "Bill, will you call someone to clean this up while I get my aunts settled? Oh, and will you tell Claude that there will be four of us for dinner?"

He nodded, shrugging off her thanks, while Mark stood grinning at the two small women. His smile faded when Valerian turned to him.

"Young man, there's a *Ficus benjamina* in there that's getting too much water. Tell somebody. It'll be dead in a month!"

"And a *Fatsia japonica* right next to it," Primrose added earnestly. "That little waterfall is drowning it."

Kim got the two of them settled in a small suite and waited while they changed their damp clothes. "Don't get me wrong," she said, watching them shake drops of moisture from their hair. "It's wonderful to see you, but what are you doing here?"

Primrose looked up. "In the city, the hotel or the ferns?"

"All three."

"Matt said to drop in whenever we wanted," Valerian reminded her, smoothing a dark skirt over her skinny hips. "We thought this was as good a time as any."

"That actor's grandma is fading fast," Primrose added. "So, we figured we'd visit you and—"

"Be able to get a direct flight to Los Angeles as soon as we hear something about the funeral," Valerian finished.

"And the ferns?"

Primrose took up the story. "Once we got here we didn't quite know how to announce ourselves so we decided to look around. We met an interesting little man with a strange name and talked with him for a while."

"Then we saw the ferns," Primrose added. "Actually, it wasn't the ferns that interested us, it was the *Ficus* and the *Fatsia japonica*. They looked quite nice filling in an empty spot, but they simply didn't belong."

Kim nodded, understanding. It made perfect sense. That would have been all that was necessary to make the aunts step nearer to the plants—and after a bit of discussion to walk in amongst them for a closer inspection.

"And the lovely flowers you sent us? Thank you very much by the way, but is there some . . . *reason* for them?"

"Ah." Valerian and Primrose exchanged a swift glance then smiled at her. "We just . . . thought you should have them."

"Svelte."

Primrose pronounced the word with satisfaction. The four of them were eating dinner in the exclusive little restaurant tucked away on the main floor, and she was looking at Kim. "Yes, child, you are positively svelte. Your mama had a sweet tooth and carried a bit of extra weight, but you don't have to worry."

"Oh, look!" Valerian nodded to a table in the corner, smiling at a short dark man sitting next to a slender blonde. "There's Ornery, that nice little man we met earlier." She turned to Matt. "Although why a mother would name an innocent little baby Ornery is beyond me."

Matt barely glanced around. "Henri is back," he told Kim quietly. "He's the one who called a while ago."

Kim's nod was preoccupied as she tried to pull her thoughts away from the two baskets of flowers. "What did he want?"

"His job back. And whatever else he could get."

Hawthorn, she mused. Those were the white flowers in Matt's basket. And yellow celandine and dock. "What did you tell him?"

Matt shrugged. "What do you think? I told him he could have his job, but the restaurant is yours. Forever." Dismissing the topic, he turned to Valerian. "How did your neighbors take the news about the Beaumont place?"

Valerian speared a piece of chicken and chewed it thoughtfully. Swallowing, she said, "Pretty much as I thought they would. They have a lot of questions." She grinned at him. "For now, though, they're trusting Kim to keep you in line."

White chrysanthemums and pansies, Kim itemized silently. Black poplar leaves and angelica. The four plants in her basket. She blinked thoughtfully, absently listening to the others.

Primrose nodded. "They want to talk to you sometime soon. The only problem with that is Miller's market will be too small. We'll have to find another place to meet. Will you come back to Posy Creek?"

Kim looked up. Her eyes widened at the blaze in Matt's eyes. A second later it was gone.

"Sure." His voice was noncommittal. "Anytime." Changing the subject, he asked, "Did that old lady you were talking about ever..." His voice died away.

"Pass on?" Primrose said helpfully. "Monty Murphy's grandma? Not yet." The two women looked at each other.

"That Ornery fella seems like a nice young man," Valerian said, directing another smile at the far table. "But he isn't easy to understand. Even though he was speaking English, I sometimes had the feeling we were speaking a different language."

Kim's heart jumped. Language. Was that one of the missing bits? And the expression in Matt's eyes just now? Was that another?

In the language of flowers, she mused, feeling her way slowly, hawthorn meant hope. And the bright yellow celandine spoke of joys to come, the dock for patience. Was that Matt's message from her aunts? Patience, hope and joy?

And hers? Pansies were for thought, angelica for... inspiration. Poplar for courage. And chrysanthemums? For what? For *truth!* Her pulse jolted as the bits began to fall in place.

"Dessert," Primrose twittered. "Oh, my, just look at that dessert cart. Should we? What do you think?"

At best, Kim reflected, her aunts' logic could be described as convoluted; at worst, chaotic. But sometimes in their own peculiar way they had a better understanding of a situation than other "normal" people did. They saw through the pretense, the self-protective devices that most mortals used to shield themselves. Sometimes they were wrong. But damn it, quite often they were right!

With their typical disregard for subtlety they were urging her to evaluate the situation and have the courage to be honest.

"Kim?" Matt's warm hand wrapped around her wrist.

"Hmm?"

His eyes smiled and he repeated what her aunt had said. "Dessert? What do you think?"

Kim knew what she thought. That she loved Matt to distraction and she wanted him to be happy. Not just so-so happy; all out, all the way, no-holds-barred happy.

She also thought that maybe she had been wrong these past couple of weeks—maybe Matt didn't want what she thought he wanted. And maybe she had been too afraid of making a mistake to try to find out!

And just that quickly, as she had done the day they had met, she tossed all logic, all caution, all deliberation out the window.

"I think—" she said with a smile that made him blink "—that I'll trade you a restaurant at the top of Kingsley Towers for one in Posy Creek."

It was very late the next morning when Matt opened his eyes. Deciding that a glimpse of Kim first thing in the morning was worth a second look, he closed and opened them again. She was sitting up, leaning against the headboard, the sheet pooled at her waist, fiddling with the remote control. When his hand gripped her thigh she smiled down at him.

"You're awake."

He pulled himself up beside her and dropped a kiss on her left eyebrow. "It just looks that way. I've really died and gone to heaven. Which means it's a convenient time for a funeral since your aunts are in town."

She shook her head. "Wrong. They took a commuter flight to L.A. at the crack of dawn."

Matt's brows rose. "The actor's grandma?"

"Yep. They heard last night. The funeral's today."

"And they're really going to crash it?"

"They're going to try."

Matt smiled, ignoring the newscaster's voice in the background. "I wish them luck." Then his voice grew serious. "Last night, what made you do it?"

"Remember the story The Gift of the Magi?" she asked thoughtfully. "The young man sells his watch to buy a barrette for his wife's hair, and—"

"She sells her hair to buy him a watch fob," Matt finished quietly.

Kim looked up at him. "I had to know if that's what we were doing. If I was wrong—oh, wait, listen!" Kim turned the volume up to hear the newscaster.

"—Monty Murphy's family and close friends say goodbye. Murphy's grandmother was buried at a private service this morning." The camera panned the crowd of rich and famous leaving a small chapel.

Kim clutched Matt's arm. "Look!"

Two elderly women, looking small and frail in their black dresses and furs, wept softly into their hankies.

"They did it." Matt was astounded.

"That's Gregory Nash behind them. He's supposed to be Murphy's best friend. As well as a star in his own right." Kim suddenly stiffened. "Oh, my God."

The camera zeroed in on a burly giant who had *security* written all over him. He squinted at a list in his hand and scowled at the two old women, then stalked over to them. Four blue eyes widened over two hankies, and the two ladies tottered to a standstill. When Gregory Nash bumped into them they delicately collapsed against him, still peering over the white linen. The movie star took one look at the pathetic duo, put an arm around each of them and swept them along with him, frowning ferociously at the hapless guard. When the two women smiled up at him with identical expressions of tearful worship, he patted them gently on the shoulders.

Matt hugged Kim and roared with laughter. "God, that was priceless." He wiped his eyes. "I wonder if I can buy a copy of that tape."

"Get two," Kim chuckled, resting her head on his shoulder. "And give one to the aunts for Christmas." She looked over at him suddenly serious. "Matt, if you're sure—"

"I'm sure."

"—then I think you should give the restaurant back to Henri."

"*What?* He left me with only eight hours' notice!"

She patted him soothingly. "I don't think he'll ever do anything like that again." She chuckled. "Gerda has a good head on her shoulders. She won't let him."

"I'll think about it."

"Good. While you're thinking," she directed, "think about when you want to get married."

He didn't hesitate. "Now."

"You *knew* I was going to marry you, didn't you?"

"You had to," he said simply. "One way or another, you had to."

Kim touched his mouth with gentle fingers. Yes, she had to. "By the way, I want you to know I'm not welshing on our deal. I'm still going to give you a damn fine restaurant."

"You better."

"And I want to invite Margo and Jock to the wedding."

"Fine."

"Matt?"

"Mmm."

"I think you should make Mary an executive of some sort and let her take over some of the things you do around here."

His brows rose. "It's an idea," he agreed.

"And when things get too quiet in Posy Creek we can come back here in the helicopter and have a night on the town."

He grinned, loving it, loving her. Her mind was working at top speed and her tongue wasn't far behind. But there was still one question he needed answered. "Last night. What made you think I wanted—"

Kim stopped him. "Bits and pieces. The flowers. Things you'd said. And when Aunt Primrose asked you if you'd go back to Posy Creek, you got the same look in your eyes that you get when you look at me. Hungry," she added, sparing him the effort of asking.

Matt rolled her over and stretched out beside her. "Starved," he corrected, dropping a hard kiss on her parted lips. "By the way, last night I made love to you last."

"We made love together," she pointed out.

He shook his head. "No, I remember distinctly. You made love to me, then I made love to you. Then we went to sleep. So, lady," he said lazily, "you owe me."

Kim slid over him and sat up, bracing her hands on his broad shoulders. Her silky hair flowed down, sliding over his chest, and her green eyes laughed down at him. "Well," she said softly, "that's easy enough to fix. Because you know, Matt, I always pay my debts."

* * * * *

Bestselling author NORA ROBERTS captures all the
romance, adventure, passion and excitement of Silhouette in
a special miniseries.

THE
CALHOUN WOMEN

Four charming, beautiful and fiercely independent
sisters set out on a search for a missing family
heirloom—an emerald necklace—and each finds
something even more precious . . . passionate romance.

Look for THE CALHOUN WOMEN miniseries
starting in June.

COURTING CATHERINE
Silhouette Romance #801

July
A MAN FOR AMANDA
Silhouette Desire #649

August
FOR THE LOVE OF LILAH
Silhouette Special Edition #685

September
SUZANNA'S SURRENDER
Silhouette Intimate Moments #397

CALWOM-1

Silhouette Books®

IT'S A CELEBRATION OF MOTHERHOOD!

Following the success of BIRDS, BEES and BABIES, we are proud to announce our second collection of Mother's Day stories.

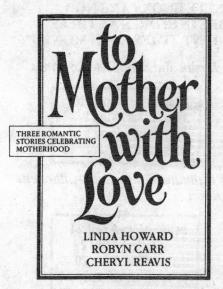

to
Mother
with
Love

THREE ROMANTIC
STORIES CELEBRATING
MOTHERHOOD

**LINDA HOWARD
ROBYN CARR
CHERYL REAVIS**

Three stories in one volume, all by award-winning authors—stories especially selected to reflect the love all families share.

Available in May, TO MOTHER WITH LOVE is a perfect gift for yourself or a loved one to celebrate the joy of motherhood.

Silhouette Books®

ML-1

Silhouette Books®

SILHOUETTE BOOKS ARE NOW AVAILABLE IN STORES AT THESE CONVENIENT TIMES EACH MONTH*

Silhouette Desire and Silhouette Romance

> May titles: April 10
> June titles: May 8
> July titles: June 5
> August titles: July 10

Silhouette Intimate Moments and Silhouette Special Edition

> May titles: April 24
> June titles: May 22
> July titles: June 19
> August titles: July 24

We hope this new schedule is convenient for you. With only two trips each month to your local bookseller, you will always be sure not to miss any of your favorite authors!

Happy reading!

Please note: There may be slight variations in on-sale dates in your area due to differences in shipping and handling.

*Applicable to U.S. only.

SDATES-RR

Take 4 bestselling love stories FREE

Plus get a FREE surprise gift!